Dead Night
(Kiera Hudson Series Two)
Book 1.5

Tim O'Rourke

Dedicated to The Potter Fans!

More books by Tim O'Rourke

Vampire Shift (Kiera Hudson Series 1) Book 1
Vampire Wake (Kiera Hudson Series 1) Book 2
Vampire Hunt (Kiera Hudson Series 1) Book 3
Vampire Breed (Kiera Hudson Series 1) Book 4
Wolf House (Kiera Hudson Series 1) Book 4.5
Vampire Hollows (Kiera Hudson Series 1) Book 5
Dead Flesh (Kiera Hudson Series 2) Book 1
Dead Night (Kiera Hudson Series 2) Book 1.5
Dead Angels (Kiera Hudson Series 2) Book 2
Dead Statues (Kiera Hudson Series 2) Book 3
Dead Seth (Kiera Hudson Series 2) Book 4
Dead Wolf (Kiera Hudson Series 2) Book 5
Dead Water (Kiera Hudson Series 2) Book 6
Witch (A Sydney Hart Novel)
Black Hill Farm (Book 1)
Black Hill Farm: Andy's Diary (Book 2)
Doorways (Doorways Trilogy Book 1)
The League of Doorways (Doorways Trilogy Book 2)
Moonlight (Moon Trilogy) Book 1
Moonbeam (Moon Trilogy) Book 2
Vampire Seeker (Samantha Carter Series) Book 1

Author's Note

I wrote this book for the 'Potter' fans and it's my way of thanking all of you for following Kiera and Potter as they try to figure out why the World has been pushed. Without you guys there wouldn't be a story as there would be no one out there to read it. So thank you.

However, I just wanted to take this moment to thank someone else, who if I didn't have working away quietly in the background, these stories wouldn't be possible. That person is my wife Lynda and she puts up with a lot. She gives me the time to write. But not only that, Lynda is my fiercest critique. I call her my 'Hacker'! Lynda is the person that reads the stories I write before anyone else and she is brutal. For such a quiet lady, she sure knows how to voice her opinion when it comes to the stories that I write.

I remember while working on 'Vampire Hollows', I spent eight hours one Sunday writing, and in that time I produced about 6,500 words. Feeling happy about what I had written, I gave it to Lynda to see what she thought of it. She handed it back to me with her thoughts written down the margin. Some of these thoughts included the phrases. *"Tim, this is shit!", "Tim, are you on acid?", "Tim, this isn't good enough!"* In fact, the whole days' work was edited out of the book. I sulked like a big kid at first. And I think we even had a crossed word or two – but the thing is, Lynda was right. Those 6,500 words did slow the story, they weren't relevant and did have to go. Lynda gets rid of the flab (and I'm not talking about my waistline!). She gets rid of the excess and keeps me in my place. Over the last year, Lynda has 'hacked' thousands and thousands of words from all of my books and I think I will add a new section to my website so you can read what was taken out.

Not many people know this, but I was actually going to kill Potter off at the end of Kiera Hudson Series One – but Lynda said that if I did she would divorce me and there's a little bit of me that believes she would have (I think she loves Potter more than me!) I never tell her what I'm going to write, or about any of the twists that I'm going to work into my stories, so when Lynda read the part where Kiera's mum ripped out Potter's heart, I was getting really dreadful looks from across the room. But I knew what was coming, so I wasn't heading for the divorce courts – not just yet anyhow!

Thanks Lynda for everything and for saving Potter!

1

Potter

Hallowed Manor spiralled away beneath me. I disappeared into the clouds, and I was glad that I had lost sight of that building - and Kiera, too. I loved the girl, but she drove me half-crazy most of the time. How could someone so beautiful be such a pain in the arse at times?

With the wind rushing over me, I banked left and sped away. It felt good to be flying again – doing what I was meant to do. I couldn't be stuck on the ground for too long – that was another thing that drove me fucking nuts. Since coming back from the dead I felt...I dunno...how did I feel? That was the problem. My head was a shed and I couldn't think straight. It didn't help that I'd been trapped like a caged animal in that manor for the last six weeks or so. I'd had to listen to Kayla's whining, Isidor's stupid comments, and then there was Kiera. What was her problem? Not for one moment did I think coming back from the dead would be like living in an episode of the Walton's – but Kiera had gone cold on me – shoved me aside.

I'd really hoped that now that Luke was dead, we would have become closer. But we hadn't. It felt as if we were growing apart. But the thing that really pissed me off was that feeling I had inside again. Those gut-wrenching feelings I had felt when Sophie had told me to fuck off. That feeling as if I wasn't any good – a monster, a freak. Maybe I was? But I hadn't expected Kiera to go cold on me and that hurt more than Sophie's rejection. Sophie was scared of me because I was a monster beneath my flesh – but Kiera was like me – well, almost. She was a monster too – so having her turn her back on me at night, roll away to the furthest corner of the bed, pissed me off.

To lie next to Kiera and not be able to have her drove me insane. And it wasn't just a sex thing, to be close to her, to hold her in my arms, to feel her soft black hair against my chest, had made coming back from the dead liveable. I felt that with each passing day, Kiera was growing further and further away from me, and I didn't know how to hold on. And she was keeping secrets, too.

The cracks – yes I had seen them as I spied through the gap in the bathroom door one morning a few weeks ago. I watched her strip naked and I had to stop myself from kicking the bathroom door open and grabbing hold of her. But, it was as I wrestled with my cravings for her that I saw those cracks appear in her skin. I had seen some weird stuff, but nothing like that. Her skin had turned old-looking, like it was covered in a web of wrinkles. Kiera's soft white skin had turned grey – the colour of stone. She looked like an ancient statue that had been left standing for hundreds of years in the baking sun. Her skin looked dry, cracked, and as rough as sandpaper.

Before Kiera caught me spying at her through the gap in the door, I had sneaked back to bed and pulled the sheet over me. I didn't want her to know that I had been spying on her – she would have made me pay for that. But, with the sheet over my head, I wanted to shut out those images of her. They reminded me too much of that statue I had seen in the grounds of Hallowed Manor.

And where in the freaking hell had that come from? What was it? Was it really a girl made from stone who was somehow moving around the grounds of the manor when not being watched, like Kiera believed it to be? The world had been *pushed* – but that was taking the piss.

The world wasn't the same one we had left. We had come back to one that was similar, but different. I understood Kiera's desire to want to find out why we had been brought back, but running around the place like Miss Marple on crack wasn't the way. The only way to find out what had happened to the world while we had been dead was to leave the manor and *push* back.

With no sense of direction as to where I was heading, I drifted through the clouds. My wings stretched out on either side of me, and the need for the red stuff was that one constant itch that I just couldn't quite scratch. Lot 13 helped – but not much. There was nothing like the real stuff. How long I could keep going on that pink shit Ravenwood had dreamt up, I didn't know – but either way, it was soon going to run out. Kayla and Isidor were drinking it like it was going out of fashion. And what happens once it's gone? Another reason to *push* back - and fast. But where would I find the answers? I didn't know anyone in this world anymore. I'd only really had one true friend and that had been Murphy, but he was dead now.

I circled in the air, the clouds dampening my skin and hair. Everything seemed so quiet up here. It was the peace I had been looking for. I'd had plenty of time to think lately, sitting alone by the fire in the gatehouse; but away from the manor, my thoughts seemed clearer somehow. The gatehouse had become my hiding place away from the others. It was where I sat, smoked, and looked into the fire. I thought of my past life and wondered why the Elders had brought me back from the dead. Sometimes, as the fire hissed and spat in front of me, I felt like screaming over and over again. The crazy stuff about the world being pushed I could take to be honest. I couldn't give a rat's arse what Disneyland was now called – but I knew things ran deeper than that and if I needed any proof of it, I thought of Kiera standing alone in front of that mirror – her flesh cracked and smashed-looking.

"You are an angel now, Sean Potter," the Elder had whispered from the blackness.

"Potter," I whispered back, feeling totally disorientated and hung over. "People call me Potter."

"Gabriel is your new name," a voice had said, and this time it was different from the last – a different Elder. In the Dust Palace, their voices had sounded like kids, but here, in the utter blackness, their voices were deeper, rasping, and old-sounding.

"Give me a break," I had whispered, my throat feeling dry and scorched.

"We are giving you a break, Gabriel," another of them spoke.

"Potter," I cut in.

"We're giving you a chance to go back," the first Elder

told me, its voice so deep that my whole body seemed to rattle.

"Go back?" I asked, straining to see through the darkness. I couldn't see or feel anything. It was like I was weightless. "Go back where?"

"Above ground," one of the Elders thundered.

"Why?"

"Kiera will need you."

"Kiera?" I said, trying to move closer to the voices. "Where is Kiera?"

"On a mortuary slab," one of them said, and I was sure that I could hear the faintest sound of a chuckle come from one of them.

"A mortuary slab?" I groaned with fear.

"The post mortem is nearly done," the first Elder said, its voice now taking on some urgency. "You don't have a lot of time."

"Time for what?" I pushed, just wanting to stand up. Was I lying down? I couldn't be sure. I could've been wandering around with my thumb up my own arse for all I knew. I couldn't feel anything.

"You want to help Kiera, don't you?" one of them whispered in my ear, and I flinched away.

"Yes, what do you think?" I tried to snap, but my throat still felt raw.

"The others are ready to go with you," it whispered again, but this time in my other ear.

"What others?" I asked. Then added, "Not her mother, she killed me, right? I think that puts the whole interfering mother-in-law thing into perspective. I don't think we're going to see eye to eye you know, especially..."

"Even in death you're a wise arse," another of the Elders boomed.

"So who are these others?" I asked.

"Friends," the Elder replied its voice softer now.

"I don't remember having many of them," I said, not trying to be funny this time around.

"Kayla Hunt and Isidor Smith," the Elder who was hovering around my ear whispered.

And how ever much I wanted to make a flippant comment about them, I couldn't. They were my friends. I tried to fight it, but I couldn't help but feel a spark of excitement in my stomach at the thought of seeing them both again.

"Where are they?" I asked.

"Outside the *mortuary*," one of them said. "They are waiting for you."

"Well, what are we waiting for?" I said. "Best get me up there before Isidor tries to blow the place up and Kayla drives everyone to suicide with her constant whining."

Then, as if I were being dragged backwards through a tunnel, a wall of wind rushed past me. But I wasn't actually moving anywhere; it was the Elders swooping around me, hidden beneath their flowing robes. As they flew close, I could smell them, and they smelt old, like meat that had been spoilt. They smelt dead. Like my eyes were being opened for the first time, I looked upon the faces that hovered just inches from mine. Their flesh stank and I could see why. Beneath their hoods their faces were a criss-cross patchwork of scars. Some were open and raw-looking and others had been crudely stitched closed. Whoever had done it must have been freaking blind. The thick, black stitching had been weaved not only into their cheeks, lips, ears, and eyelids, but had been sewn into the fabric of their hoods. The wounds looked rancid, and oozed thick, gloopy puss like tears onto their disfigured cheeks. Their eyes were white, like they had been rolled back into their sockets.

A wind blew hard around us, causing their robes to fly open like tattered-looking wings. I caught a glimpse of their pale bodies. Not much made me want to puke ever, but what I saw beneath those robes caused hot bile to gush into my mouth, like I'd been sucking the acid from a car battery. The two male Elders' chests were open, held together with lengths of black cotton. Their upper torsos looked like an old boot which had had its laces tied together loosely. Through the stitching, I could see their hearts, and they were black and withered, like prunes that had been sucked dry. They pulsated slowly, beating behind a ribcage that was covered in stringy pieces of dead flesh.

"You like what you see, Gabriel?" one of the female Elders asked, reaching out and dragging one gnarled finger down the length of my cheek.

It wasn't the time to start bitching about my name, so I stayed quiet. Her broken fingernail felt like an ice-cold razor as she curled it around my chin and over my Adam's apple.

"Don't pity us," she whispered, her face next to mine. "We have known such pleasure and now it is time to share it with you."

Before I'd had the chance to say anything, it was night and I was standing in the rain. There was a streetlamp overhead, and the rain glistened in its orange glow. My long, black coat flapped around me, and at first I thought my wings were open.

"Hey!" someone hissed, and I turned around to see Isidor pointing his crossbow at me.

"Put that down before you kill someone," I snapped, my throat no longer feeling raw.

"I didn't realise it was you," Isidor said, lowering his crossbow.

"Who else did you think it would be?" I hissed. "You often see people suddenly appear out of thin air?"

"I guess not..." Isidor started.

"Where's Kayla?"

"Don't you mean Uriel?" Isidor asked me.

"What are you talking about?" I barked, "And I thought you had problems before you died."

"That's what the Elders called me," Kayla said, appearing from beneath the dashboard of a nearby parked car.

Then, remembering how the Elders had called me Gabriel, I glanced at Isidor and said, "And what did they call you? It couldn't be any worse than..."

"Maliki," Isidor said proudly.

"You've got to be kidding me," I spat.

"And what about you?" Isidor asked me, the rain dribbling through his black hair and running down the length of his face.

14

"Potter," I said.

"Don't tell lies, Gabriel," Kayla called out as she lay wedged beneath the dashboard of the car. "They told me that was going to be your new name."

"You must have heard wrong," I snapped.

"Yeah, maybe it was Gabriella," Isidor said, staring at me. I couldn't tell if he was being thick or just taking the piss.

Ignoring him, I turned to look at Kayla's butt sticking out of the car and said, "What are you doing?"

Then, before she'd had a chance to say anything, the car rumbled into life. Kayla climbed from the car, and looking at me she said, "Stealing a car, of course. How else are we going to make our escape?"

"Escape from where?" I asked her.

"There," she said, pointing in the direction of a nearby building.

I looked through the driving rain to see a grey brick building on the other side of a small car park. Written on a sign that was attached to the side of the building were the words:
County Mortuary

"Kiera," I breathed, heading towards the building, knowing that she was lying somewhere inside on a cold slab.

"You wait with the car," Isidor said, raising his arm as if to block me.

"And who put you in charge?" I asked, eyeing him up and down.

"We've been here longer than you, Gabriel," Kayla smiled, and I caught her wink at Isidor. "We've had a chance to check out the place. Kiera is being worked on in a room on the other side of that door," she added, pointing to a large double door which was big enough to reverse a hearse into. "Wait with the vehicle."

"I think I should..." I started.

But before I'd had the chance to finish what I was about to say, Kayla and Isidor were racing across the car park towards the door set into the side of the building.

I took a pack of cigarettes from my coat pocket, and cupping my hand around the tip of it so it didn't burn out in the rain, I lit it. Leaning against the boot of the car, I watched Isidor and Kayla reach the door. It seemed that they both had everything figured out and well planned, and I wondered if being murdered and brought back from the dead hadn't made them both grow up a bit. Then, watching Isidor raise his boot and smash the door in, I guessed that dying hadn't changed them at all.

As I circled around and around, the sky grew darker. Night had begun to draw in. I still had no idea how I was going to find out what had caused the world to be *pushed,* and what other changes had taken place, other than my favourite band changing names. But I knew that I wasn't ready to go back to Hallowed Manor just yet. Kiera seemed to have her plans and I needed to formulate some of my own. I wasn't intending to set myself up in practise as some private investigator, just on the off chance that a mystery might come along that could lead us to finding out what had happened to the world while we had been away. I loved Kiera, but the whole thing sounded too much like an episode of Scooby-Doo to me.

But with Murphy gone and my only true friends enclosed behind the walls of Hallowed Manor, who else did I have to help me? Who else did I know in this world that could tell me what had happened while we had been away? Then, as I looped in the air, I thought of the only other person who had ever meant anything to me: Sophie. But the last time I'd ever seen her she had been peering back at me over the top of her bed sheet. I remembered the fear, revulsion, and hatred for me in her eyes.

"Get away from me!" she'd screamed, kicking out with her feet. "You freak – you animal! Get out!"

"I love -" I'd begged.

"GET OUT!"

So, jumping from her bed, where only moments before we had been making love, I went to the windows. Throwing them open, I climbed onto the ledge. I looked at her, two perfect green eyes staring back at me, and to see such fear in them had broken my heart.

"I'm sorry," I'd growled.

Then, leaping from the window, I spread my wings and shot into the night sky. I hadn't looked back, not once. It would have hurt too much to do so.

But that was then, I told myself. Things were different now – the world was different. Would she even recognise me? Had that part of her life – the life that she had shared with me as a Vampyrus - been wiped away, just as the Elders had wiped away all the Vampyrus who had lived in secret amongst the humans? There was only one way to find out.

With my wings pointed outwards, I back flipped in the air, then raced towards the Earth.

2

Sophie

I hadn't been a pathologist for very long, but even so, I had never seen a corpse sit up in the lab and go stumbling out into the night. The police officer had been taken into the main hospital building, screaming. His face had been the colour of ash, eyes bulging from their sockets as he begged the medical staff for pain relief.

"Fix my legs! Please somebody do something! Fix my legs!" he had cried, as he was bundled onto a stretcher and taken away. The lab assistant, although not physically injured, had been taken away by the police officers who had arrived. They wanted to undertake an interview but I guessed by the state of him that he wouldn't have made much sense at all.

"She came back to life! She came back to life!" The lab assistant had kept mumbling to himself over and over again. "She just got up and walked right outta here!"

"What about you?" one of the officers had asked me.

"What about me?" I'd asked right back.

"Are you okay?"

Scraping my hair behind my ears and re-knotting my ponytail, I simply nodded and said, "I guess so."

"What happened here?" the officer asked.

"I'm not sure," I said.

"Look, whatever took place, we're going to need to speak to you," the officer said, pulling his notepad from his shirt pocket.

"Can't it wait?" I had asked, yanking the latex gloves from my hands, rolling them into a ball, and throwing them into a nearby bin. "I need to tidy this place up and get my thoughts together."

"You can get your thoughts together, but not here. This place needs to be locked down. It's a crime scene now," the officer informed me.

"A crime scene?" I asked, bewildered and not thinking straight.

"Whatever took place here tonight, several things are clear: We have a suspected murder victim missing, a lab assistant jabbering on about a walking-talking corpse, my skipper has two broken legs, and frankly, you don't look too good yourself. So taking everything into account, and until we have a clearer picture of what's gone on, this place is being shut down. Okay?"

Nodding, I looked about the lab. The metal mortuary table stood lopsided against the wall and for the first time, I noticed the tiles were cracked and broken behind it. The cracks in the wall ran vertically and I realised that was where the police sergeant had been standing when the *corpse* had rammed the table against him.

Had she really pushed the table so hard against that officer's legs that the sheer force had smashed the tiles in the wall behind him?

I couldn't believe it. That would've been impossible. Wouldn't it?

She would've had to have had the strength of...

It was then that I noticed the corpse's blood samples that I had requested for DNA and blood group analysis. The blood looked black, like undiluted blackcurrant squash, bottled in a thin plastic tube. Without thinking, I moved towards the counter on the opposite side of the lab where it sat.

"Where do you think you're going?" the officer asked me.

I had forgotten that he was there. Snapping my head around, I looked back at the officer.

"I'm getting my coat, is that okay?"

"Sure, no worries," the officer said. "Just don't touch anything."

Turning, I moved across the room, my eyes fixed on the vial of blood that had been siphoned from the corpse.

I need to get that blood tested. It might be the key...the code...to that woman who seemed to be able to grow her fingers and face back.

Conscious that the police officer was scrutinising my every move, I made my way to my office which was next to the counter that contained the blood. Entering the office, I removed my white lab coat and placed it on my desk. I took my own coat off the hook on the back of the door and hung it over my arm. Back in the lab, I looked at the officer who continued to watch me.

"Ready?" he asked.

"Yeah...no hang on a minute...where's my mobile phone?" I said, taking the coat from over my arm and placing it on the counter, concealing the bottle of blood with it. Then, I searched the pockets of my coat as the officer stood and watched. Glancing over my shoulder, I smiled at him and said, "Oh, here it is. It was in my coat pocket the whole time. I'd be lost without it. How did we manage before the damn things were invented?"

"Dunno. Can't remember," the officer said. "Can we just hurry it up? Scenes of Crime officers are waiting to get in here."

"Oh yeah, sorry," I said, scooping up my coat, hiding the bottle of blood in the folds of its material. "I'm good to go."

The police officer ushered me out into the cold night air, and it was nice to be out of the lab.

"How do you put up with that smell?" the officer asked me, steering me towards a police car.

"What smell?" I asked, realising where I was being guided to.

"Disinfectant!"

"Oh that," I said, the officer pulling open one of the rear passenger doors to the police car and motioning for me to climb inside. I clutched the bottle beneath my coat. "I'd rather ride in my own car, if you don't mind?"

"I'd rather you came along with me," the officer said, stepping aside from the door so I could get in.

"My car's just over there, officer. How am I going to get back from the station when I've finished giving you my statement?"

"Not to worry. I'll drop you back when we're done," he assured me.

Stepping away from the door, I said, "That's very kind of you, officer, but I'd still rather..."

"I insist," he said, a fake smile tugging at the corner of his lips.

Then, with a fake smile of my own, I said, "Am I under arrest, officer?"

"No."

"We'll then, I'd rather travel in my own car." Turning away from him, I made my way towards my car, which sat in a pool of orange light from the streetlamp above.

"I'll follow you to the station," I said. As I climbed into the driver's seat I saw his face, he was looking at me with suspicion.

Does he know about the bottle? No, if he did he would have stopped me by now.

I pulled the driver's door closed with a thump, placed my coat on the passenger's seat, and watched him through the windscreen. The officer stood by the open door of the police car.

He suspects something. He's gonna come running over here any minute and arrest me...arrest me for what? For removing evidence from a crime scene – that's what!

It was then I saw his eyes as he stared at me from beneath the streetlamp. In the warm orange light, his eyes seemed to glow a fierce yellow and I knew then that he was a Skin-walker – once a wolf but now matched with a human.

Trembling, I forced the key into the ignition and the car rumbled to life. The police officer then climbed into his own vehicle.

What evidence have I taken? I wondered. *Evidence that perhaps that corpse wasn't completely human? But then again, neither was that cop.*

I watched as the taillights of the police car glowed like burning coals. Then, I eased forward and followed the officer as he swung his car away from the kerb and drove out of the hospital grounds.

Keeping my eyes on the car in front, I searched the folds of my coat for the bottle. I closed my fingers around it. It felt warm. I knew that if it were to be any good for testing, I would have to get the blood sample into refrigeration - and quick.

But where? Not home. I can't take a detour back there. That would definitely raise the officer's suspicions. Besides, that was mum and dad's house, and I didn't want them to get involved in this.

The police car swung out onto the dual carriageway and I followed.

Marty! I could take it to Marty's. He could test it for me!

As if driving on autopilot, I followed the officer. Marty seemed the natural choice. We had broken up six months ago and I had gone back to live with my parents. We had met while at medical school. I had studied pathology and Marty, the human genome. But what would his reaction be to me turning up on his doorstep in the middle of the night, clutching a bottle of blood?

We hadn't spoken for six months and the last time hadn't been pleasant. Pleasant? Who am I trying to kid – it had been downright nasty.

I eased up on the gas, letting the gap between my own car and the police car grow.

He'd never gotten over the fact that I'd been awarded custody of Archie.

I let the gap grow further still.

Archie had always loved me more than him anyway!

The gap grew.

Hadn't it always been me who had taken him to the park?

The police vehicle slowed and narrowed the gap.

Archie's mine...

I eased down on the accelerator. I didn't want the officer to get suspicious.

Would he still be bitter about Archie after all this time?

I looked ahead and saw the police car's left-hand indicator winking on and off, casting long orange shadows across the tarmac.

Only one way to find out!

I waited for the police officer to commit himself to the slip road, then, thumping my foot down on the accelerator, I sped away down the carriageway, leaving the officer behind.

3

Sophie

"What do *you* want?" Marty asked me, pulling his dressing gown about him.

I looked at his hair. It stuck out at the sides in untidy clumps like a clown. For the first time, I noted the grey streaks weaved amongst the dark brown curls and wondered how long he had had them. He was twenty four like me, way too young to be going grey. His face looked worn, and his cheeks and chin were covered in a spray of whiskers that protruded from his face like needlepoints. Lines had appeared around the corners of his eyes. Deep creases had formed around his mouth and streaked across his forehead. It was these that now wrinkled as he looked at me standing on his front step.

"I said, what do you want, Sophie? It's nearly three-thirty in the morning."

Pushing past him, I stepped out of the cold and into the hall.

Closing the door, Marty said, "Sophie you can't just turn up out of the blue like this and barge your way in." Then, rolling his eyes towards the ceiling, he added, "I've got company."

"You always had company, if I remember rightly," I said with a wry smile.

I made my way to the rear of the house and sat down at the kitchen table. Marty followed me and switched on the kettle. "This had better be good, Sophie. I don't appreciate you turning up like this."

"You're not still mad at me about Archie, are you?" I asked.

"I'd been trying to forget about him," Marty told me, and heaped two teaspoons of coffee into mugs that he had snatched from the sink. "It hurts less when I try not to think about him."

"If he meant so much to you, how come you haven't

even paid him a visit in over six months?"

Then, clutching the coffee cup to his chest he said, "That's why you're here, isn't it? Something's happened to Archie. Oh my god what's happened to him?"

"Calm down," I soothed. "Nothing's happened to Archie."

"Are you sure? You're not trying to break it gently to me, are you?"

"For crying out loud, Marty!" I sighed. "There's nothing wrong with Archie. He's perfectly okay."

Marty splashed hot water into the mugs and brought them over to the table. He sat opposite me and pulled a pack of cigarettes from the pocket of his dressing gown.

"Thought you'd packed them in?" I said, sipping the sweet, hot coffee.

Popping the cigarette between his lips, he lit it. "I've started again, okay?"

"When?" I asked, watching him over the rim of the mug. It was then I remembered why I'd hated him smoking so much, it reminded me of someone else – someone I had once been scared of – but I just couldn't remember who, however much I tried.

"About six months ago. About the same time you stopped me from seeing Archie," he explained.

"You know those things will kill ya," I started.

"Please, Sophie, spare me the lecture."

"Look…" I began.

"No, you look. Archie was my dog. It was me who saved him from that rescue centre. You didn't even want a dog," Marty argued.

"Yeah I did. I've always been a dog lover," I argued back.

"Yeah whatever!" Marty said, squirting bluey-grey smoke from his nostrils. "I'm not gonna sit here arguing about Archie at this time of the morning."

"You started it," I said.

"No I never – you did!"

"Didn't," I spat.

Pitching out his cigarette, Marty sighed, "I take it you didn't come all the way over here in the middle of the night just to bitch about Archie?"

"No," I said.

"So what do I owe the pleasure, *Sophie*?" and he said my name as if he had just swallowed something disgusting and it was creeping back up his throat.

"I need you to do something for me," I said, and this time my voice softened.

Pulling another cigarette from the pack, Marty grimaced. "I don't believe you! I haven't seen you in over six months and you suddenly show up expecting favours."

"Look, Marty, I wouldn't have come all the way over here if it weren't important."

Drawing on his cigarette, Marty eyed me and said, "You in some kinda trouble? What is it, a man?"

"No it's not a *man!*" I huffed.

"Well if it's not a man, what is it?"

I put my coat on the table and unrolled it. Then, picking up the capsule of blood, I held it out in front of me. The blood sloshed up the sides of the bottle and it looked thick and black.

"What's that?" Marty asked, eyeing the bottle with surprise.

"What do you think it is? It's ice cream!"

"I meant *whose* is it?" Marty asked.

"That's the favour," I told him. "I want you to test it for me."

"Test it for what, exactly?"

"Everything you can think of," I said, rolling the vial across the table towards him.

Dangling the cigarette between his lips, Marty flicked the bottle back across the table at me. "Test it at your own labs."

"I would if I could, but I can't," I told him.

"Why not?"

"I just can't, okay," my voice starting to sound scared.

Marty sensed my fear and picked up the bottle. He eyed the blank label which ran down one side of it where the patient's name should have been written.

"What's going on, Sophie?" Marty asked, crushing the

cigarette out in the ashtray with his finger and thumb.

"I don't know," was my honest reply.

How can I tell him about what's happened tonight? About what I've seen and from where that blood sample came from? Who that sample came from!

Marty rolled the bottle between his fingers. "I'm sorry, Sophie, but I'm not…"

"I'll let you see Archie," I cut in, hating the desperation in my voice. "You can have him at weekends. He'd love to see you – his *daddy.*"

Marty gripped the specimen bottle in his fist and stared at me. He didn't speak.

"I could bring him over on a Friday night and pick him up…"

"How do I know you'll keep your word?" Marty asked.

"I promise, Marty. Test that blood for me and I'll…"

"Okay! Okay!" Marty said. "I'll do it."

"It has to be done straight away," I explained. "I need those results like yesterday."

Marty looked at the bottle, then back at me. "What's so important about this blood?"

"That's what I'm hoping you will find out," I said.

As if knowing that he wasn't going to get any answers from me, Marty stood, crossed the kitchen, and placed the sample into the fridge. I got up from my seat, and turning around, he jumped to find me standing right behind him. Before he knew what was happening, I had leant forward and planted a gentle kiss on his mouth.

Touching his lips with the tips of his fingers he looked at me and said, "What was that for?"

"It's to say thank you."

"Very cosy," someone said from the opposite side of the kitchen.

Both of us turned to see a female, wrapped in a fluffy blue bathrobe standing in the doorway. She had auburn hair that hung about her shoulders and brilliant green eyes – just like mine.

Had he replaced me?

Marty leapt away from me as if I were about to bite at any moment and said, "Jenny, it's not what you think!"

"You pig!" Jenny screeched and stormed from the doorway.

"Jenny! Jenny!" Marty shouted at her. The sound of her feet rumbled like thunder as she marched back upstairs. Marty looked back at me and snapped, "See the trouble you've caused!"

"Sorry," I said, biting my lip to hide a smile.

Shaking his head, Marty went to the foot of the stairs. "Jenny, my love – it's just Sophie, my ex..."

Crash! The bedroom door slammed shut.

I followed Marty to the foot of the stairs.

"What do you want now?" he groaned.

"Your sofa," I smiled.

"What are you talking about?" Marty asked, starting off up the stairs.

"To sleep on. I can't go home just yet."

"No!" Marty shouted without even looking back at me. *"No way!"*

"Just for tonight, Marty. I'll be gone first thing in the morning. I promise."

Then, from the darkness of the landing, I heard his voice, tired and exasperated. "Do whatever you want, Sophie. You always did!"

Stepping away from the bottom of the stairs, I went into the living room, which we had once both shared. Stretching out on the sofa, I listened to the muffled sounds of Marty and Jenny arguing from above.

"Whoops!" I smiled as I drifted off to sleep.

That had been six weeks ago, and now I was on the run.

4

Potter

To be honest, I didn't know whether hooking up with Sophie again was a good move or not, but I couldn't think of anyone else – I didn't know anyone else. The last time I had seen her, she looked shit-scared of me, and although I hadn't thought of Sophie for some time, whenever I did, that memory of her peering over the top of her bed sheet at me and screaming wasn't a nice one.

What about the letters I had sent her? After leaving her that night, I had written several times but Sophie had never answered. Why not? Because in her eyes I was a monster- *a freak* – that's what she had called me. And what would Kiera think if she knew who I was looking up? Was Kiera the jealous type? Sure she was. She hadn't liked Eloisa hanging around me much. But I was doing this for Kiera. I just wanted to find out what had happened to the world while we had been dead. That's all I wanted from Sophie. It wasn't like I had feelings for her anymore. That was a part of my life that had been pushed – *pushed* right away.

The last time I knew Sophie, she had been living with her parents and had been studying music. She played the piano, and played well. Maybe she was some famous pianist now…or maybe not? What did she now do in this world that had been pushed?

I raced through the air, soaring above the clouds so as not to be seen from the ground. The evening was turning out to be a cold one, but at least the rain had stopped. Circling above the town of Ripper Falls, which was on the western and most southern tip of England, I shrugged my shoulders so my wings rolled back, and I dropped through the night sky like a stone. Beneath me I could see Sophie's parents' house and I wondered if she still lived there with them. The house was set away from the rest of the town on a remote piece of farmland that her father had inherited from his grandfather, if I remembered rightly. The farm was surrounded by fields and in one of them I spied a scarecrow.

Landing in the field just feet away from it, my wings disappeared into my back and I crossed the rain-sodden earth towards the scarecrow that lent over to one side. Its face was a cloth sack that had been stuffed with straw, making it look way too big for the rest of its body. It stood in a crucified position, and as I approached it, several crows that perched on its outstretched arms squawked at me. I shooed them away with a flap of my hands. Being stripped to the waist, I couldn't very well go strolling up to Sophie's parents' house half-naked and ask if I could speak with their daughter. The scarecrow had been dressed in a long, black raincoat, so I took it and put it on. It was filthy dirty and torn in several places. I looked at myself in the long, dark coat and knew that either way, stripped to the waist or wearing this flasher's mack, I looked like a pervert. But it would have to do. Pulling the coat tight about me, I headed through the dark towards the house which sat in the distance.

A spiral of smoke curled up from the chimney, and I could see the orange glow of light through the windows. As I drew near, a dog started to bark wildly from within the house. There was a stone wall and a white wooden gate set into it. It wailed on rusty hinges as I pushed it open and the dog's barking became wilder. As I approached the front door, I hadn't even had a chance to knock when it flew open and a shotgun was thrust into my face.

I recognised the man at once to be Sophie's father. He looked older than I had remembered him. His eyes were circled with grey smudges and he looked as if he hadn't slept in weeks. What was left of his hair was white and it stuck up all over the place, as if he had gone mad with a tub of hair gel.

"Whoa, old man!" I said, raising my arms in the air to show him that I wasn't any threat. "Take it easy – don't get so excited!"

Ignoring me, Sophie's father shoved the end of the gun under my chin. God, what had been his name? I couldn't remember now.

"Who are you?" he asked me, and I could sense his fear. I glanced at his finger and I could see that it was pulling on the trigger.

"I'm a friend of Sophie's," I told him, and tried to smile.

"Bullshit!" he hissed, and a black Alsatian came tearing into the hall behind him. The dog barked at me, its jaws ferocious-looking.

"Quiet, Archie!" Sophie's father roared. The dog snarled at me and raced around its master's legs, its tail flicking to and fro. Once the dog had quieted down, Sophie's father looked down the barrel of the shotgun at me and said, "Sophie doesn't have any friends."

"I went to college with her," I tried to explain, my hands still raised.

Eyeing me with suspicion, he said, "Oh yeah, what college was that?"

How the fuck should I know? I wanted to say, and even though I was already dead I didn't fancy a face full of shot. "What was it called?" I said thoughtfully.

"What did she study?" he came back at me.

"Music," I said confidently, knowing this to be true.

"Liar!" he roared. "You've come for her, just like the others." There was a flash of white light along with a booming sound as I flew backwards through the air.

I lay on my back in his overgrown garden and my chest felt hot, like a burning poker had been rammed between my ribs. Then, there was another booming noise as Sophie's father slammed the front door shut. I opened my eyes and stared up into the night sky. The stars seemed to spin above me and I groaned in pain. I placed my hands to the gunshot wound and could feel a ragged hole in my chest.

"The son of a bitch shot me," I coughed, as blood rushed up my throat and into my mouth. Rolling onto my side, I dragged myself to my knees. I opened the front of the scarecrow's coat and looked at the hole in my chest. It was black and scorched-looking, and blood pumped from it in a black stream, which ran down over my stomach. Leaning forward, I gritted my teeth and forced my thumb and forefinger into the wound. Blood rushed over my hand in a cold stream. Blind, I felt for the tiny lead balls that Sophie's father had pumped into me. One by one, using my fingers like tweezers, I pulled them out, and I couldn't help but wonder why the parents of my girlfriends all wanted me dead. Was I really that bad?

With all the shot removed, I staggered to my feet, the sound of the dog barking from inside the house echoing out across the surrounding fields. With the hole in my chest starting to congeal over, I went back to the front door. But this time I didn't even think about knocking. Raising my foot, I put the door in. It flew off its hinges and shot up the hallway in a spray of splinters. The dog bounded into the hall and raced towards me. With my own fangs out, I snarled back at the dog. Seeing me looming in the doorway, claws raised and fangs glistening, Archie made a whimpering sound and raced away back up the hall.

"You call yourself a guard dog?" Sophie's father roared as he came running back into the hallway. Then, seeing his front door lying in splinters and his dog pissing up the lampstand, he looked at me. "What in the name of sweet Jesus is going on -" he started. But before he had a chance to get the rest of his words out of his mouth, I was on him.

Pinning him to the wall, and with my fangs just inches from his face, I ripped the shotgun from his hands and said, "Is Sophie here?"

"But I shot you," he gasped, looking at me as if I were some kind of ghost.

"And it fucking hurt," I hissed. "So don't do it again, it's not very nice."

"But you should be dead!" he cried, and again I could see the fear in his eyes. "You're a Skin-walker, aren't you?"

Then, realising that I should be keeping my Vampyrus form hidden, I looked away and withdrew my fangs. "Yes," I whispered. "I am a Skin-walker."

"I knew it," he breathed, trying to wriggle free from my grip on him. "You're just like the others."

"What others?" I asked, looking back at him.

"You know," he said, sounding breathless. "You're one of them. You want Sophie."

"Where is she?" I asked him, tightening my grip, not understanding myself what was really going on. Why would Skin-walkers be looking for Sophie? And what the fuck were Skin-walkers anyway? If I were going to find anything out from Sophie's father, I would have to get him to trust me, to understand that he had nothing to fear from me, nor did his daughter.

"You don't recognise me, do you?" I asked him, lowering my voice, but still keeping hold of him. He'd already shot me once and hadn't even blinked.

"I've never seen you before," he mumbled.

But we had met before. He hadn't liked me much, but we had met before – before the world had been *pushed*. But I didn't exist in this new world; no Vampyrus did and never had. I was a complete stranger to him and I guessed I would be a complete stranger to Sophie, too.

This was now a world full of Skin-walkers, as he called them. It was full of scared men like Sophie's father, who thought little of killing any complete stranger who came to his front door asking to speak with his daughter. He had never been like that in the world that I knew and remembered. Sophie's father hadn't been a desperate man. He had been quiet, respectable, and a lawyer. The sort of man that was shit-scared of his own shadow, not a man who went brandishing a shotgun in your face.

If he had changed so much, what about Sophie? How different would she be? If her father didn't recognise me, then she wouldn't either. The time that we had shared together had never taken place in this world. I had never existed – never been a part of her life. The Sophie from this world hadn't studied music – she didn't play the piano – she was different. So what, then, was the point in trying to find her? She didn't know me and I didn't know her. I'd find out as much from Sophie as I would a complete stranger on the street.

Why then had I come looking for her? Did I really believe that she would remember me? And if she had, would she have even wanted to know me? I'd come looking for her because I wanted to find something familiar in this strange, new world. I wanted something to connect me to my past. Although I had spent years above ground, it wasn't really my home. The Hollows was where I truly belonged, but they had been shut off to me now. I was the only Vampyrus left. My only true friend, Murphy was gone.

Realising how freaking stupid I'd been to even consider coming back to find some small chink of my past life, I let go of Sophie's father. He slumped against the hall wall. I looked into his eyes and smiled to myself. How could I have expected him to remember me, yet I couldn't even remember his name? I turned my back on him and walked back down the hallway towards the ruined front door. The dog lay whimpering on the floor.

Just as I was about to step back out into the night, Sophie's father called after me. "You're not like the others who came looking for my daughter," he said.

"How do you figure that?" I asked back, looking over my shoulder at him.

"The two who came before you were far more dangerous," he said. "I could see it in their eyes. Killers, they were. You're crazy, but you're not a killer."

"How can you be so sure?"

"Because I shot you," he said, "and you've left me standing."

Looking straight at him, I said, "The only reason you're still standing, is because although you don't remember me, I was once in love with your daughter."

Then, turning away, I left him standing alone in his hallway, Archie the dog licking his boots.

5

Sophie

When I awoke the following morning on Marty's sofa, both he and the girl – couldn't remember her name now - had gone. With my mouth tasting like road kill and my brown hair sticking out like I'd been dragged through a bush backwards, I climbed the stairs to Marty's bathroom. After taking a pee, I ran myself a bath. Kicking off my clothes, I strolled into what used to be mine and Marty's bedroom. His iPod was sitting in the dock that I'd bought him last Christmas. I switched it on and started to listen to *Mama Do The Hump* by Rizzle Kicks. Swishing my butt to the music, I threw open his wardrobe. Pushing his shirts and trousers to one side, I smiled to myself on seeing that there were a few of my own clothes left hanging from the rail. Ah bless, he hadn't been able to throw them out. Taking a sweater and a pair of my old jeans from the rail, I jumped backwards.

It was the box. It sat there on the top shelf of the wardrobe. It was the shoebox, the one with the letters in it. They were the letters which had ultimately ended mine and Marty's relationship. I had set fire to them. I had destroyed them in front of Marty to prove that they didn't mean anything and that I had no idea who the sender had been. But the letters had kept coming. As soon as I had destroyed one, another arrived in the post the following day. The address on the front was always the same, smudged and unreadable. Only my name was legible – written in the spidery scrawl that covered the envelopes and inside pages. How the postman knew where to deliver the letters was a mystery. I had taken to waiting for the letters to arrive and when I heard them land on the mat, I would race into the hall and yank open the front door – but there was no postman outside or anywhere to be seen in the street.

The letters at first made Marty smile. He believed they were from some secret admirer of mine. But he soon became pissed off, as the letters became more personal. I lost count of how many times I tried to convince him that I didn't know the identity of the letter writer, but some of them were so personal that even I began to wonder if I hadn't in fact known him in some other life – some other time perhaps. But that would have been impossible. The saddest thing about it all was the fact that, while those letters were partly responsible for ending my relationship with Marty, they were the most beautiful love letters I had ever read. They were so full of warmth, sadness, and yet in places, anger. The sender spoke of the love that we had shared, but over and over again he asked for my forgiveness – he was sorry that he had scared me. What could he have done to have scared me so much? I didn't even know him.

Sitting on the edge of the bed that I had once shared with Marty, I took the lid from the old shoebox and peered inside. As I feared, the box was full of those envelopes, with the address smeared in black ink across the front of each of them. But I had destroyed these letters over and over again. Had more arrived since I'd left? Taking one of the letters from the box, the smell of stale tobacco smoke wafted from the dog-eared sheets of paper inside. I looked down at the untidy scrawl and the letter was identical to the one that I had been sent so many times before – the same letter I had ripped up, burnt, and flushed down the toilet a hundred times. I didn't need to read the letter. I knew whole passages by heart. Turning it over in my hands, I looked down at the signature and wondered if I would ever find out who the sender really was. He always signed the letters *"Potter."*

The song by *Rizzel Kicks* finished, and I could hear the sound of water sloshing into the bath tub. "Shit!" I gasped, hoping that the water hadn't overflowed onto the bathroom floor. I placed the letters back into the box and hurried down the landing. The water lapped around the edge of the bath, and I turned off the taps just in time. Releasing some of the water, I lowered myself into the tub and laid back. Closing my eyes, I thought of those letters again and wondered who "Potter" was. Maybe they were intended for another Sophie, that's what I had always told myself and Marty during the arguments that we'd had over them. Marty had become convinced that I'd been having an affair with this Potter. It didn't matter how many times I tried to convince him that I'd never even known anyone with that name, let alone could have slept with him, Marty never really believed me. I could see the suspicion in his eyes as he peered at me through the smoke that curled up from the tip of his cigarette. And sometimes in that smoke, it was like someone was staring back at me. Whoever it was scared me. His eyes were jet-black and it was like they were boring right into me.

Then, just after Christmas, Marty got drunk and slept with someone else. He cried when he told me, and said that he had wanted to get his own back on me – he had wanted to hurt me like those letters had hurt him. I had left that night, taking Archie with me. I had gone back to my parents. And in some way, even though I didn't know this Potter, there was a small part of me that blamed him for mine and Marty's break–up. Why had he sent me those letters? I had never been in love with him.

With my head sinking beneath the bath water, I wondered why those letters had still kept coming – the same letters saying the same thing. They were old and tatty-looking, as if they had been written hundreds of years ago. Suddenly, a hand gripped my shoulders and pulled me from beneath the water.

"Where did this come from?" Marty shouted at me, holding the vial of blood that I had given him the night before.

Even though we had once been lovers, I folded my arms across my breasts and shook the water from my hair. "Hand me a towel," I said.

Marty threw one at me. Holding the glass tube of blood just inches from my face, he hissed, "Where did this blood come from?"

"What do you mean?" I asked him, stepping out of the bath and wrapping the towel around me.

"Don't act dumb, Sophie," Marty snapped, and there was a look about him that I had never seen before. Marty looked scared.

"From a corpse that was brought into...." I started.

"Was it human?" he shouted, coming towards me, the tube still gripped in his fist.

"Of course the blood came from a human," I told him, thinking of how it had regrown its face and fingers, then sat up and walked out of the mortuary. I didn't tell him that though; maybe when he calmed down a bit.

"Don't lie to me, Sophie!" he yelled, his eyes growing dark. "This isn't human blood – not any human that I've ever examined."

"What are you talking about?" I said, brushing past him and heading back to his bedroom where I had taken the clean clothes from the wardrobe.

"This blood isn't like any other species that I've come across," he shouted, following me into the bedroom. "I ran some tests on it and the closest species of animal I could find is the Desmodus Rotundus."

"Speak English, please," I said back, tugging on my jeans and pulling the sweater over my head.

Then, almost seeming to shove the tube of blood into my face, he said, "This blood has come from something very similar in species to a bat – a vampire bat, to be precise."

Dragging my hair into a ponytail, I looked at him, then at the blood and said, "You must be mistaken, it came from a young woman..."

"What woman?" he breathed.

"She was murdered..."

"I want to examine the body," he said, gripping my arm.

"Ouch!" I gasped, snapping my arm away. "You're hurting me, Marty!"

"I want to see the body that this blood came from..." he started.

"You can't," I said, rubbing my arm.

"Why not?" he barked at me.

"Because she sat bolt upright on the slab then did a disappearing act out the door with some guy holding a crossbow and a young girl with red hair."

"Stop taking the piss, Sophie and just tell me..."

"Who's taking the piss?" I snapped back. "It's you who's standing there telling me that the blood I gave you has come from a vampire bat."

"Something close to a vampire bat," he corrected me. "It's like whoever this girl was, she was half-human and half..."

Then, before he'd had the chance to finish what he had started to say, there was a thumping sound on the front door below.

"Who's that?" I gasped, the sudden sound shocking me.

"Take the blood," he said, shoving it into my hands. "Whatever you do, keep it hidden – keep it *safe!*"

"Marty!" I called after him, as he headed down the stairs.

The thumping sound came again.

"Who is it?" I heard Marty call out.

"Open up!" I heard someone shout from the other side of the door.

"What do you want?" I heard Marty yell, his voice wavering as if full of fear.

Then the air filled with a crashing sound as the front door was torn from its hinges.

"Get out of here!" Marty screeched.

"Where's the girl?" A deep-throated voice boomed.

Not knowing what to do with the tube of blood, I placed it into the box with the letters and replaced the lid. On tiptoe, I crept onto the landing and peered over the edge of the banister. All I could see was a long, drawn-out shadow cast against the hall wall. It towered over Marty, who stood looking up, as if whoever the shadow belonged to was a giant.

"Sophie Harrison," the voice roared. "Where is Sophie Harrison?"

Hearing my name being spoken, my heart began to race and the hairs at the base of my neck started to prickle.

"I don't know anyone called Sophie..." Marty started.

"You lie," the voice cut over him.

Crouching, I peered through the banisters, desperate to see who or what was searching for me. The shadow, which stretched up the hall wall, bent forward, as if leaning over Marty. Then, the hallway seemed to burn yellow with a warm glow.

Skin-walker? I wondered. I knew that they could control you with their eyes. I'd heard that their eyes could glow with such intensity that they could set alight the eyes of another, just by staring at them.

There was silence from downstairs. It was so quiet that I could hear my own heartbeat. Then, I heard Marty speak and I froze.

"Sophie's here," he said, his voice so flat and emotionless, he sounded as if he were dreaming. "Sophie is upstairs," he added. Then he began to scream.

The shadow I had seen spill across the hallway moved and headed towards the foot of the stairs. I crawled backwards and into the bedroom. As quietly as I could, I pushed the door closed and stood up.

Where was I going to hide? I screamed inside as I scanned the room for any possible hiding place. I could always hide under the bed. The Wardrobe? But whoever was climbing the stairs in search of me knew I was up here and it would only be a matter of time before they found me. No, I had to get away from the house. I raced around the edge of the bed, my legs feeling as if I were running in quicksand. With my hands shaking, I fumbled at the window lock. From behind me, I heard the bedroom door swing open. Glancing over my shoulder at the figure in the doorway, I screamed at the sight of Marty.

His eyes burnt yellow in their sockets as if they had been set on fire. But he didn't seem to be in any pain as he smiled at me. I stared at him as he slowly closed the bedroom door and turned to face me.

"Marty?" I murmured, now so scared that I could hardly speak. "What's happened to you? Your eyes..."

Smiling, he came towards me, his eyes fixed on mine. "My eyes are fine," he said. "Don't worry about me."

"Who was at the door?" I asked him, sensing that everything wasn't fine and there was something very wrong.

"Oh, don't worry about him, he's gone now," Marty said, loosening his shirt as if he were planning on getting undressed.

"What are you doing?" I asked him, edging away.

"Don't look so scared," he said, slowly closing the gap between us. "You have nothing to fear. We used to be lovers once."

"Piss off!" I shouted, pressing myself against the wall, I had nowhere else to go. "That was a long time ago."

"Oh, Sophie," he smiled and ran his tongue over his lips. "Don't be like that. I'm not going to hurt you."

"Keep away from me," I whispered as he came within an inch of me. Although I knew that I was making a big mistake, I couldn't help but look up into his eyes. Why had they changed colour? Why were they yellow?

"Who was the girl that woke up in the morgue?" he asked me, his voice soft – almost caring.

"I didn't know her name," I tried to lie, but as I looked into his eyes, I felt my fear ebbing away. And although deep inside of me I knew that I was in danger, I couldn't help but want to trust him somehow. He was Marty after all.

6

Sophie

He ran a finger down the length of my face and then slowly dragged it over my bottom lip, the nail slipping into my mouth and brushing over the tip of my tongue. Part of me wanted to bite down on that finger and tear it off, but another part of me wanted to take his hand and cover it in soft, sensual kisses.

"See, I'm not going to hurt you," he whispered in my ear, and I could feel him slip one hand into my hair and pull me close, his eyes never breaking free of mine. Then, in his bright yellow eyes, I saw us – like we had been before – before the letters, the distrust, and his affair. We were making love on the bed and I was crying out. His naked muscular body was pressed over mine as I pulled him into me. Those memories reminded me of how good we had been together; how sweet the sex had been. I watched us make love in his eyes; I wanted to feel like that again. I wanted to feel that ecstasy once more.

As I stared into his eyes, I could feel Marty leading me across the room towards the bed. "Who was the girl that came awake in the morgue?" he whispered again, his breath hot against my neck.

I wanted to say her name and even though I now wanted Marty more than I'd ever had, there was a voice screaming inside of me:

Don't tell him her name! Don't tell him her name!

Then, as Marty lowered me onto the bed and began to kiss my mouth, I sighed and closed my eyes. In the darkness I saw someone else and it wasn't Marty. Part of me was scared of him, but another part of me loved him. He was handsome – like a god. But it was too dark to see him clearly and in the fleeting glimpses, I was sure that he had wings. They weren't white like that of an angel, but black like some prehistoric bird of prey. His hands were strong as they cupped my breasts and his teeth felt sharp as they brushed up against my neck. His chest and stomach were as hard as stone as he lowered himself on top of me. My heart raced with fear but my body, my soul, exploded with pleasure as he made love to me.

Then he was gone in a flutter of shadows and Marty was whispering in my ear again. "What was her name?"

I opened my eyes, and the yellow light streaming from Marty's eyes was almost blinding. And I knew that it wasn't him I wanted – it was the other – the one I had seen in the darkness – the winged man, the smoker, the letter writer, Pott....

"Her name?" Marty asked again, and this time the softness had gone out of his voice, he had started to sound frustrated with me. I didn't want Marty to touch me anymore. I just wanted him to be away from me. His touch repulsed me, made me want to gag.

"Hudson," I whispered, in his ear. "She told me her name was Kiera Hudson and that she was one of the Dead Flesh."

Hearing this, Marty began to chuckle. I'd never heard him laugh like that before, it sounded old and rasping like an old man coughing on a throat full of pipe smoke. As if waking from a dream to find my ex-boyfriend taking advantage of me, I pushed him away. He didn't resist. Marty climbed to the edge of the bed where he sat and laughed.

"So at last she has come back," he grinned to himself, his eyes spinning in their sockets. "Kiera Hudson has returned."

"You knew her?" I asked, moving away from him up the bed, feeling confused and furious that Marty had been kissing me.

Then, turning to face me, he said, "I knew Kiera Hudson. Of course I did. I was the person who murdered her."

"You're scaring me, Marty," I murmured, scrambling off the bed. "What do you mean you murdered her?"

But before he'd had the chance to say anything, someone started to scream from below.

"I'm blind!" the voice screeched. "He's made me blind!"

Even though the voice was high-pitched and terrified, I knew it was Marty's I heard. But that was impossible, right?

Marty was sitting at the end of the bed. Then, Marty started screaming from outside.

"What's going on in here?" I breathed, racing towards the window. I looked out onto the street below to see Marty stumbling into the road. His hands were outstretched as he clutched blindly at the air.

"Help me!" he screamed. "He's burnt my eyes out!"

Not being able to comprehend what I was seeing, I glanced back over my shoulder to Marty – the other Marty – sitting and grinning back at me from the edge of the bed.

"Marty?" I whispered at him.

Chuckling to himself, he looked at me, his eyes spinning like two Catherine Wheels in his face. "Oh, Sophie," he smiled and clapped his hands together.

The sound of screeching brakes from outside made me turn back to the window. With my hands clasped to my face, I watched the blind Marty corkscrew into the air as an oncoming car smashed into him. With his arms flapping like wings on either side of him, Marty seemed to float in the air forever, until he hit the road with a sickening thud. I span around and looked back into the room, but Marty had gone, and in his place stood a giant. Standing at least seven foot tall, he was nothing more than a thin sheet of flesh wrapped around a pile of bones. His face was long and pointed, his cheeks and eye sockets sunk deep into his face. He wore a blue denim shirt, loose-fitting jeans, and a navy blue baseball cap on his head. A red bandanna was tied about his scrawny throat. His lips looked cracked and dry, and as he smiled at me, I could see a black set of fleshy gums and a row of smashed teeth that looked as if he had been chewing on a mouthful of toffees. But it was his eyes. They almost seemed to spin in their sockets like fireworks on bonfire night.

"Who are you?" I whispered.

"It doesn't matter," he smiled as he headed for the door. "You won't remember me."

Looking at his freaky form, I said, "I won't forget you."

At the door, he turned back, and with his lips looking so thin that they looked like a crack in a plate, and his seething eyes boring into mine, he said, "Sophie, you seemed to have forgotten so much already."

Then, he was gone, and I was standing alone in the bedroom that I had once shared with...

"Marty?" I gasped. He had been trying to get it on with me – kissing me – and I'd told him to piss off. Then what had happened? I looked at the dishevelled bed. I'd pushed him off me and he had run from the room.

"What a pig!" I snapped, taking a small holdall from the bottom of the wardrobe. Not really knowing what I was doing or why I was doing it, I snatched up a shoebox that was lying on the floor at the foot of the bed, and along with Marty's iPod, I placed them into the holdall.

"I can't believe it!" I fumed as I headed down the stairs. "How dare Marty think I would just jump straight back into bed with him!"

At the foot of the stairs, I saw that the front door was hanging from its hinges like a wobbly tooth. "Marty?" I called out. "Where are you?" I was still mad at him for trying to get it on with me, but something told me that there was something wrong with this picture.

The *whoop-whoop* sound of approaching sirens filled the air outside. Still clutching the holdall, I made my way from the house and into the street. A small gathering of people were at the kerb. I eased my way amongst them and to my shock, I could see Marty lying in the street, one side of his head popped open like an overripe melon. Blood gushed from the hole and turned the street black. Marty's eyes were open and they looked blankly up at the sky.

"Marty!" I cried and went to him, kneeling at his side. "Marty, what happened?" As I leant over him, I couldn't help but notice what looked like scorch marks around his eyes.

The sound of sirens was deafening now as several police cars turned into the street and came to a screeching halt. Those who had gathered around Marty dispersed like people did when police arrived. I stayed beside Marty, and even though I knew he was dead, I wasn't going to leave him.

"All citizens are to clear the street!" a police officer ordered through a speaker attached to the police car. "Clear the street!"

Looking up, I could see that I was now alone with Marty. The doors to the lead police car swung open and two officers got out. They were huge, wedged into their military-style uniforms.

"Move away from the body," one of them barked as he came towards me, a long, black pointed Taser in his hand.

"He was my friend," I said, trying to fight back the tears standing in my eyes.

"Get away from the body," the cop ordered again, firing up his Taser stick. Blue and mauve sparks sizzled and crackled from the end of it.

"Please," I started, hoping to reason with what was left of the human soul hidden beneath the skin. I looked up into the Skin-walker's eyes.

Then, looking down at me, the officer said, "I know you. You gave me the slip last night on the way back from the morgue. We've been searching for you everywhere."

Recognising the officer, I looked away as if trying to hide my face, but I knew it was too late for that. "I think you must be mis -"

"You're under arrest," the officer barked before I'd even had the chance to finish.

"For what?" I asked him, hearing the sound of other officers approaching me from all sides, their Taser-sticks crackling.

"For theft of evidence relating to murder," the officer said.

"What evidence?" I asked, although I knew he was talking about the blood – the blood that was lying in the holdall by my side.

But when the officer spoke again, he didn't accuse me of stealing the blood; he accused me of stealing something far more bizarre and insane.

"You stole the body of that young woman," he said, dragging me to my feet. His grip was strong, and I could feel his fingernails sinking into the flesh of my upper arm.

"Are you kidding me?" I gasped. "How in the hell did I steal that body? What did I do, stuff her up my sweater?"

"You had accomplices who came in and took her body away..."

"Accomplices?" I spat as he dragged me towards one of the parked police cars. I gripped the holdall, refusing to let go of it. "Ask the lab technician and that other copper – the one with the broken legs."

"Impossible," the officer growled. "Both of them are dead."

"Dead?" I breathed. "How?"

"Sergeant Banks died of his injuries," the officer said, steering me towards the rear door of his police car.

"People don't die of a broken leg," I said, trying to resist as he forced me onto the back seat of the car.

"He did," the officer snapped at me, his eyes glowing bright.

"And the other one?" I asked him. "What happened to him?"

"Suicide," he replied. "Very sad. Whatever he witnessed in that morgue disturbed his mind so much that he..."

"This is bullshit!" I yelled, knowing that I was being lied to. I didn't trust Skin-walkers at the best of times – let alone one in a police uniform.

Drawing my knee back, I kicked out at the door as he tried to close it on me. Then, there was a burning sensation which travelled up the length of my leg. I jerked my leg backwards and cried out in pain. The cop waved his Taser-stick in front of my face and with a look of hatred for me, he said, "Next time I'll zap you straight in the face."

With tears streaming down my face, I curled up on the backseat and held my leg. The pain was excruciating and made me feel sick. The smell of burnt flesh filled the car. I heard the officer climb into the front seat and fire up the engine. Another climbed in beside him, but I was in so much pain, I didn't even look up.

"What about Marty?" I said through gritted teeth.

"Marty?" the happy-zapper officer said.

"My friend," I whispered.

"The guy you murdered, you mean?" he asked, looking back over his shoulder at me.

"I didn't murder him!" I groaned, the pain in my leg sapping any fight I had left in me.

"Not what several witnesses have told us," he said, pulling away from the kerb. "Apparently you pushed him right out in front of that car."

"They're talking shit," I whined, holding my leg.

"And you're in it," the officer said, and the other copper laughed.

7

Potter

I must have been mad to even consider the idea of going in search of Sophie. What was wrong with me, for crying out loud? It was like I was in some kind of emotional shoot-out or something. Part of me was glad that she hadn't been home. But there was that other part – the part that feared for her safety. Sophie's father said that others had come looking for her and that they'd been killers. Why would these people be looking for her? What kind of life was she leading now in this world that had been *pushed*? Sophie had been the kind of girl who wouldn't have said shit even if her mouth had been full of it – so how had she got herself into trouble? And what kind of trouble was she in?

Was it my problem? No – not really. We had been lovers once and I had been in love with her – but she had rejected me. Even when I'd left her bedroom that night, as she lay screaming and petrified of me, I hadn't been able to forget – not at first, anyway. As I had crisscrossed the country picking up the odd job here and there and sleeping in cheap motels, I had written to her. In each letter I had explained in the best way I could – and I wasn't very good with words – how much she had meant to me and how sorry I was for scaring her. But Sophie never replied once. She made it clear that she didn't want anything more to do with me. So why should I go and get myself into a heap of shit for her now? I attracted shit like a cow's arse attracted flies and I didn't need it, not now. I was meant to keep my head down in this new world. Kiera had said that – and she was right.

Kiera! What about Kiera? She needed my help more than Sophie did. I needed her help too. Perhaps I shouldn't have left the manor? Kiera and I were a team now – we always had been. I turned my back on Sophie's home once and for all, knowing I would never mention that I had come looking for

Sophie – whatever my true reasons had been for doing so. Then, leaping into the air, my wings shot from my back and I raced into the cold, winter sky. I didn't head straight for Hallowed Manor; I was going to take a detour first.

Kiera had stuff that she wanted, especially her police badge more than anything. So banking right, I headed in the direction of Havensfield.

I knew Kiera's home address, but I had never been there. She had spoken about her flat to me many times, talking about her comfy armchair placed by the window so she could sit and watch people pass by in the street below. Kiera had told me about the thousands of newspaper clippings that covered her living room wall. As I flew nearer to Havensfield, my curiosity grew about how Kiera had lived and what her life had been like before leaving for The Ragged Cove.

The streets of Havensfield were deserted, and just a few houses still had lights shining within them. It was late; I didn't know how late, but I guessed that most people had gone to bed for the night. That suited me, as I didn't want to be seen by anyone, especially as I was breaking into Kiera's flat. I just wanted to get her stuff and get back to the manor.

Swooping out of the sky, I felt my wings withdraw into my back and wrap themselves around my ribcage. I'd had wings for as long as I could remember, but I could never get used to that feeling of them disappearing back into me. Every time it happened, it felt like I was momentarily suffocating. Then my lungs would expand, and I could breathe again.

I pulled the collar of the scarecrow's coat up about my throat, glanced up and down the deserted street, then approached the front door that would lead me to Kiera's flat. Without much effort, I pressed my shoulder against the door and felt the lock pop. With one last look over my shoulder, I eased open the door and snuck inside. There were three doors leading off the main hall, and a staircase leading up into the darkness. Knowing that Kiera lived in flat number four, I climbed the stairs. I tapped gently on the door with my knuckles, just in case Kiera had been evicted, and in her absence somebody else had moved in. I waited several moments and when I didn't get any response or hear any movement from inside I pressed my shoulder against the door and forced it open.

I closed the door behind me and stood alone in her flat. It felt odd being there on my own. In a weird way, it felt like I was, invading Kiera's private space. But I'd only returned to get her badge and some clothing. The place was in darkness, and I couldn't risk turning the lights on. The flat had stood empty for months or more, and it might make neighbours curious if they suddenly saw a light on in the flat.

Feeling my way across the poky living room, I wondered where Kiera might have left her police badge. There was a door set into the wall and I pushed it open. A bed was in the far corner of the room and it looked like the bed clothes were lumpy and dishevelled, as if Kiera hadn't made her bed the last time she had slept in it. Smiling to myself, I headed towards a small nest of drawers. There was a bedside lamp, and what felt like a book and a jewellery case. Running my fingertips amongst the clutter, I couldn't find Kiera's police badge. So, opening the top drawer I began to rummage around inside. It seemed to be full of clothes of some kind. Still in search of Kiera's badge, I removed some of the garments. Then, holding a piece of clothing that felt elasticated, I realised I was looking through the darkness at the biggest pair of women's knickers I had seen in my life.

"Whoa, Kiera," I breathed, struggling to picture her wearing such frumpy underwear. They were nothing like the skimpy, silky numbers I had seen Kiera wear. I pulled out another pair. "Jeez, I never knew you wore parachutes!"

Then, from behind me I heard someone scream. "Who are you?"

Wheeling around with the giant-sized underwear in my hands, I saw the silhouette of a figure sitting up in the bed, and it was then I knew that I was in the wrong flat. The bedside lamp flickered on to reveal an old woman sitting up in her bed.

"What are you doing with my knickers?" she screeched, her snow-white hair matted and her wrinkled jowls swinging on either side of her ancient-looking face.

"Sorry, Grandma," I gasped, sounding as shocked as her. "I've got the wrong flat."

"Help!" the old woman screamed at the top of her voice, and for such an old woman, her voice was strong and ear-piercing.

"Take it easy," I hushed, just wishing she would stop.

"Pervert!" she screeched, pulling her bed clothes up around her chin.

"I'm not a pervert," I tried to assure her, stuffing her knickers back into the drawer. "I've got the wrong flat. I thought someone else lived here."

"You're a pervert!" the old woman screamed again. "Somebody help me – there's a man in here sniffing my knickers!"

"Now hang on, Grandma," I said, unable to believe what I was hearing. "I wasn't..."

"I've read about young men like you in the newspapers," the old woman croaked. "You're one of those kinky types."

"*Kinky?*" I blustered and for the first time in my life, I was lost for words. "I'm not kinky!"

"Get out!" she screamed again.

I could hear movement from the adjoining flats. So, not wanting to be caught in the old woman's flat clutching a pair of her giant knickers, I looked at her one last time, told her I was sorry, and fled. As I raced down the stairs, a door opened above me.

"What's going on?" a man shouted, sounding half asleep.

"Pervert!" I heard the old woman screech again.

Yanking open the front door, I slipped back out into the night. Not knowing what direction to head in, I turned right, and pulling the scarecrow's coat tight about me, I disappeared into the shadows. I reached the end of the street, looked back one last time, and on seeing a man in pyjamas stagger from the flat that I had broken into, I turned the corner.

There was a covered doorway, and pressing myself flat against the wall, I waited for the man to go back inside before I spread my wings and flew away. Being discovered as a knicker-sniffing pervert was one thing, but being noticed for swooping up into the night with a set of clawed wings was something else altogether. It was as I waited in the dark for the man in the pyjamas to go away, that I noticed Kiera's beat-up old Mini parked at the kerb, just outside the doorway that I was hiding in. Turning around to see that the door to this flat was ajar, I realised the mistake I had made, so I pushed it open and stepped inside.

8

Sophie

The burning sensation in my leg began to ease, so I pulled myself up onto the backseat of the police car and peered out of the window. I'd lived in Ripper Falls all of my life and I knew that we weren't heading towards the police station. For some reason, the cops were taking me out of town and into the country. With every mile the roads became narrower and more remote. Trees grew tall and leafless on either side of the road, and between the black and twisted trunks, I could see miles and miles of desolate farmland.

"Where are you taking me?" I asked them.

The cop in the passenger seat didn't say anything; he just kept staring straight ahead. Glancing at me in the rear view mirror with his yellow eyes, the cop who had zapped me grinned and said, "Just taking a little detour."

"Where?" I pushed, trying not to look into his eyes, but wanting to know where they were taking me.

"To a little place I know," the happy-zapper cop grinned at me in the mirror. "It's nice and secluded..."

"Look, I'm either under arrest or I'm not," I said, beginning to sense that I was in serious trouble with these guys. "Either take me to the police station or release me."

"We'll take you to the police station," the cop said, "but first I thought we could have ourselves a little party."

"Party?" I breathed, but I knew what he meant and I rattled the door handle. It was locked and couldn't be opened. "Just release me."

Ignoring me, the happy-zapper glanced at the other cop and said, "I don't know about you' but human women are so freaking horny, don't you think?"

The cop in the passenger seat just grunted and stared straight ahead.

Grinning to himself, the other looked back at the road and smiled, "I've seen some beautiful female humans, but you are *lush!*" and I saw him wink back at me in the rear view mirror. "I bet you're gonna be so sweet."

I rattled the door lock again, my heart pounding in my chest. The driver saw the fear in my eyes and this seemed to excite him somehow as he twitched in his seat and straightened his trousers at the crotch. Then the other officer suddenly spoke and said, "Lady, if I were you I'd put on your seatbelt."

"Say what?" I spat.

"So you don't get hurt in the crash," he said calmly, his eyes fixed straight ahead.

The happy-zapper cop must have read my mind as he glanced at his colleague and said, "What crash?"

"This crash, you fucking animal," the cop whispered. Then with lightning speed, he shot his arm out, gripped the back of the happy-zapper's head, and drove his face into the steering wheel. A jet of black blood sprayed from the cop's face and showered the windscreen. The cop made a screeching sound and took both hands from the wheel as he tried to fight off his colleague. The back of the police car zigzagged violently across the road, and I yanked the seatbelt across my chest.

Over and over again, the cop, who had sat silently for most of the journey, drove the happy-zapper's face into the steering wheel and dashboard. The attack was relentless. Blood with flecks of flesh sprayed around the interior of the car, spattering my face and the backseat. The attack had been so sudden and unexpected that I sat rigid in my seat, unable to breathe.

The car lurched left and right across the narrow country road as the cop fought for his life. He reached for his attacker, but the other was too strong. Then, the happy-zapper cop began to change. What was left of his face began to contort and twist as if he were growing a giant snout. There was a tearing sound as the back of his shirt began to rip apart, chunks of black fur bursting through. As he changed, it was like he grew stronger too.

The other cop sensed this and roared, "Oh, no you don't, Skin-walker!" If the attack hadn't been frenzied before, the cop then went berserk as he took the Skin-walker's head in both of his hands. There was a sickening crunch as the cop crushed the Skin-walker's skull. Its eyeballs burst from its face and splattered the windscreen, like red and white jelly.

The Skin-walker flopped to one side and fell forward in his seat, the remains of his head running all over the steering wheel. The police car veered to the right and the cop reached for the wheel, but it was wet and slippery with the Skin-walker's brains and he lost his grip of it. The car spun out of control, and I was thrown sideways across the backseat. And as the car flipped onto its side and rolled into a ditch, I screamed until my throat felt sore.

I lay in the foot well, my body shaking in shock and fear. What the fuck had just happened? Why had that cop just slaughtered his colleague? What was going on here? Was he going to do the same to me? A splinter of pain cut through the right side of my ribcage and I cried out in pain as I tried to lever myself up. The car was on its side and at first I couldn't figure out which way I should head to get out.

There was a grunting sound from the front of the car. The passenger door wailed as the cop forced it open. I crawled forward, wedged between the seats, my hair hanging down over my eyes. Then, one of the back doors was yanked open, and I could feel a rough pair of hands grabbing for me.

"Get off me!" I screamed, kicking out with my feet.

"Get out of the car," the cop grunted, seizing one of my arms and pulling me up and over the backseat. He was extremely strong and within moments, I was laying on my back, next to the ditch and the upturned police car.

"Get away from me!" I shrieked at him as I tried to scuttle away. He went back to the rear of the car and pulled out my holdall. The cop unzipped it and pulled out the tube of blood.

He came towards me, holding the glass tube in his hand. He was tall and broad-shouldered. Mud from the ditch and blood from the Skin-walker covered his crisp blue uniform. He looked older than the other cop had, but it was hard to say exactly how old, as his black police cap was wedged firmly on his head, the peak pulled down so low it almost covered his face.

"Who was the girl in the morgue?" he suddenly asked me. He sounded slightly out of breath as if he were in a rush.

"What girl?" I stammered as I lay on my back looking up at him.

"I'm in no mood to play games, lady," he barked, waving the tube of blood in my face.

Why was everyone so interested in the morgue girl? I wondered. Something told me that I shouldn't tell him what I knew. I had told Marty and he was dead now. Marty told me that I should keep that blood safe – he said it had come from a vampire bat – but could that be true? With so many conflicting thoughts racing through my mind, I tried to scramble away from him again.

"Tell me her name!" he roared, taking hold of my shoulder with his free hand.

With our noses almost touching, I looked beneath the peak of his police cap and could see that, unlike the other cop, his eyes were grey with flecks of radiant blue. His lips were bloodless and pressed tightly together, and after witnessing what he had just done to his colleague, I whispered, "She said her name was Kiera Hudson."

As soon as her name had passed over my lips, the cop froze, those blue flecks flashed like lightning in his eyes.

"Who else was with her?" he demanded.

"No -"

"Who else?" he roared.

"A teenage boy and girl," I cried out, his grip now hurting my shoulder.

"What were their names?"

"I don't know!" I shouted, just wanting him to let go of me.

"What did they look like?" he hissed.

"The girl was real pretty with bright red hair," I murmured. "The boy was tall, had black tattoos up his neck and a little beard..."

Before I'd finished telling him what they had looked like he said, "Was there another with them?"

I shook my head.

"Are you sure?" he snapped. "He's in his early twenties, dark hair and black eyes. Smokes like it's going out of fashion and is a real wise guy?"

"There was no one else!" I shouted, trying to convince him.

"Are you sure?" He pushed me. "He calls himself Potter."

Then, as if being slapped across the face, my mouth fell open. For a moment everything seemed to slow down. The sound of the wind rattling through the trees and the sound of crows squawking in the unploughed fields was deafening.

Noticing the look of shock on my face, the cop shook me and said, "What is it? What do you know?"

"Nothing," I whispered, but that was a lie. I knew that the letters in the bag by the cop's feet had been sent to me by a man who called himself Potter. The cop said that this Potter had smoked. I had hated Marty smoking – because when he did, he'd reminded me of someone else – someone I had been scared of. But there was something else; my feelings were changing, too. It was like there *were* feelings inside of me for whoever this Potter was or had been. But these feelings weren't just of fear, they were of love, too. But how could I have feelings of love for someone I didn't know – someone I had never met before?

"What do you know of Potter?" the cop said, shaking me, and it felt as if I were waking from a dream.

"I don't know him," I whispered. Was that a lie? I didn't know anymore.

"Why do you look so shocked?" he came back at me, his eyes searching mine.

"You just killed a man in front of me," I gasped.

"He wasn't a man," the cop hissed, loosening his grip on me. "He was a Skin-walker – an animal, and he was going to hurt you."

"Why did you save me?" I asked him, rubbing my arm as I lay in the street. "I thought you were partners. Aren't you just like him?"

"I'm nothing like him," the cop snapped, slipping the tube of blood into his shirt pocket out of sight.

"What are you then?" I asked him.

He stared down at me and said nothing. Then, when the silence became more deafening than any noise that I'd ever heard, the cop took his gun from his belt and pointed it at me.

Inching myself away, I held my hands up and said, "Please don't kill me. I won't tell anyone about that woman called Kiera Hudson. I only told my friend, Marty, but he's dead now."

Then, coming closer, the cop shoved the gun into my hand and said, "Shoot me."

"What?" I gasped, throwing the gun into the ditch. "I'm not shooting a cop. I'm in enough shit as it is."

The cop went to the ditch, picked up the gun and went to the car. He aimed the gun at what was left of the Skin-walker's head and fired. There was a booming sound that echoed back off the fields which surrounded us on either side of the deserted road. Then, he came back towards me. Pulling me to my feet, he stuck the gun in my right hand and curled my fingers around it. "Shoot me," he said, his eyes fixed on mine.

"Are you out of your freaking mind?" I gasped.

"Shoot me," he insisted, as he wrapped my forefinger around the trigger.

"Why?" I begged, tears starting to well in my eyes. I wasn't crying out of sadness, but through fear.

"You tried to escape from the police car," he said matter-of-factly. "In the struggle, you managed to take my gun from my belt. You shot the driver in the head - by accident or deliberately, I don't know. The car crashed and you climbed free. I came after you and you shot me with my own gun."

"Please don't make me do this," I pleaded, tears now rolling freely down my cheeks.

"You've got to do this," he pushed. "I can't afford to be unmasked."

"Please..." I started.

The gun firing was like the sky being torn apart by thunder. I flinched backwards and the gun flew from my hand and clattered onto the road. The cop crumpled before me.

"Christ that hurt," he groaned as he dropped onto his back.

With my hands covering my face, I peered through my fingers at him. The cop pressed his hands against his thigh and I watched as blood gushed between his fingers.

"Why?" I murmured, not knowing what else to say. I felt numb, sick, and so scared. I had just shot a cop and he was now lying bleeding to death at my feet.

With his face as grey as the clouds above us, the copper stared up at me from beneath his cap. His eyes rolled with pain. Then through gritted teeth, he said, "Run, Sophie Harrison. Run and don't stop – not ever."

"But..." I started.

"Run! Run! Run!" he roared at me.

Snatching up the holdall, I looked one last time at the cop as he lay bleeding in the middle of the deserted road, then turning, I ran.

9

Sophie

For three days and nights I ran. On the morning of the fourth day, freezing cold and near exhaustion, I came to a small town named Beechers Hope. The sun was just a pink slip of a ribbon on the horizon, so I made my way through the desolate town. The streets were narrow and cobbled. There was a small town square with a library. I cut across the square and made my way along a tiny coastal path that spiralled upwards. There was a white-washed signpost that was partially covered by bracken. Careful not to tear my hands on the thorns, I brushed the bushes aside and uncovered the sign. *Black Hill* it read, and next to it was a faded black arrow that pointed up the side of the hill that I was climbing.

To my right, the path fell away. I looked over the edge and there was a sheer drop down the side of the cliff face to the jagged rocks below. Dark green waves crashed against them, and seagulls screeched as they circled above me. The wind was ice-cold and had a salty taste to it. My thick, brown hair blew back from my shoulders and I shivered. I didn't know for how much longer I could go without proper rest. My feet were aching and I felt filthy. I had snatched a few hours' sleep in outhouses and barns that I had discovered as I'd made my way across the country. After what had happened with those cops, I was desperate to keep away from main roads and the bigger towns. I hadn't been able to stop thinking about what had happened. During the short periods of sleep that I had managed, it had been haunted with images of that copper's head bursting open like an overripe tomato. Then there had been the other one, the cop who had forced me to shoot him, and when I would wake, the smell of gunpowder wafted on the cold air around me.

I knew that copper had set me up. He obviously had his own agenda and reasons for wanting to know about the young woman – this Kiera Hudson – who had come back to life in my mortuary and fled into the night. What was so important about her? Had what Marty discovered about her blood been true? How would I ever know now? That cop had stolen it from me. As I crossed the barren fields and navigated my way through tight valleys, I saw Marty in my mind's eye. I couldn't shake those images of him standing in the bedroom clutching that tube of blood. I would never forget the fear I had seen in his eyes as he'd told me the blood had come from a vampire bat. But I knew that couldn't be true. I had seen it being taken from the corpse's arm. But then again, she had sat bolt upright on the slab. I'd watched as her face and fingers grew back. Had she been a vampire? No, they weren't real. That was the stuff of stories – myth and legend. Just like some people believed that ghosts haunted old houses, there were some who believed vampires lived underground. I hadn't believed in any of it...but now...I didn't know what to think.

I had been raised to believe that there were only two dominant species on the planet – humans and Skin-walkers, and neither liked each other very much. Like all children, I had learnt the history of the Treaty that had been signed at Wasp Water. I had been lucky as I'd grown up, the wolves had never come to my home town, so I hadn't been taken from my parents to be matched. I'd heard stories though – that those children who had been matched were never the same. Although they looked the same, they were different once they had a wolf living inside of them. I'd never trusted a Skin-walker. It felt difficult to know that they had taken over the soul of a human, stolen their skin. It was like they were wearing a mask. All of them had something to hide, I figured. But they were a part of society – the Treaty said they had to be. They were cops, doctors, priests, politicians, generals – they had worked their way into every level of society. What had happened to me had only gone to prove that my distrust in them had been justified.

I reached the top of the coastal path to find myself standing in front of a deserted-looking farmhouse. Off to the right there stood the gutted remains of a barn, which looked as if it had been set on fire at one time. The house itself looked pretty derelict and parts of the roof had collapsed inwards. The windows were covered in thick, yellow grime and the white front door looked warped in its frame. I crossed the small area of overgrown grass in front of the farm and pushed the door with my hand. It gave a little, so I leant against it with my shoulder. The door groaned then flew open, throwing up a shower of dust and cobwebs. I didn't need to call out to know that no one was home. The place was covered in dust, and the walls were covered in black spots of mildew. It smelt musty, and as I closed the door, I was grateful to be out of the freezing wind that screamed about the eaves.

I placed the holdall on the floor, and looked about the room that I found myself in. It was small and poky, with a fireplace set into the wall. There were some dry-looking logs piled beside it. Turning around, I could see an open door that led into a kitchen. A wooden table and four chairs stood around it. There was a staircase, and slowly, I climbed it. At the top was a short landing and four doors led from it. I pushed open the first one that I came to and immediately covered my nose with my hand. The smell was repulsive. It smelt as if someone at one time had decomposed in the room. It was a smell that I had come accustomed to after opening up the dead in the mortuary. There was a double bed set against the far wall, which had a mattress on it covered in dark brown stains which looked similar to dry blood. At the foot of the bed was a wooden chair. There was a dresser against the wall, and this was covered in half-melted candles. I could also see a box of matches, which I took, along with one of the candles.

I closed the door to the room and crossed the landing. Pushing open another door, I found myself peering into what I guessed was once a girl's bedroom. There was a small bed and a faded pink blanket covered it. Next to the bed stood a nest of drawers and on top of them was a photograph and a book. I crossed the room and could see that the book was *Wuthering Heights* by Thomas Hardy. I thumbed through the pages, which were yellow and dog-eared. In the front, written in pencil, someone had scrawled the words, *Happy seventeenth birthday*

Andy – Love, Dad. Maybe I'd been wrong and perhaps the room had belonged to a boy after all. I picked up the picture and wiped a thick covering of dust from the glass to reveal a faded photograph of a young girl and a man. She was very pretty, with light blonde hair that rested on her shoulders. Her eyes were perfect blue and she had an impish look about her. The man, who I suspected was her father, was a giant. He was solidly built, with massive round shoulders. His forearms were so muscular that they looked like something Popeye would have been proud of. He had black hair that was just starting to turn grey above the ears. Unlike the girl, he didn't look happy. He looked sad – troubled – as if he had the weight of the world bearing down on those giant shoulders.

Looking at the picture caused a rush of gooseflesh to race down my back, and I put the picture back where I had found it. Wondering what had happened to the girl and her father, I left the room and went back onto the landing. I pushed open the third door and found another small bedroom. This was empty apart from a small narrow bed and a wardrobe in the corner, which looked more like a locker. Closing the door, I stepped back onto the landing and pushed open the remaining door.

I could have screamed with joy when I spotted the small bathtub in the corner. Without hesitating, I raced across the bathroom and twisted on the taps. There was a thumping sound from behind the walls as the pipes rattled to life. Then, a thick stream of brown coloured water gurgled and splattered from the taps and into the bath. As I waited for the water to run clear, I pulled off my dirty clothes and kicked them into the corner of the room. I filled the bath with water, and although it was barely warm, I sank myself into it.

I never thought I would ever be so grateful for a tub full of clean water. I sunk below the surface and let the water run through my hair. It felt as if I were being cleansed in some way. How long I stayed in the water I don't know; but when I finally climbed out, the skin covering my toes and the tips of my fingers was all wrinkled.

Heading back down the landing, I went back into the room with the bed and the faded pink blanket. I wrapped the blanket around me and
lied down. The bed was soft beneath me and I closed my eyes.

He crawled up the bed towards me, brushing his lips over the flat of my stomach and over my breasts. Although his eyes were jet-black, like two onyx gemstones, they sparkled and that smile of his crept across the lower half of his face. My heart raced and I breathed deeply. He brought his face over mine and I could feel his breath, warm against me. My whole body tingled and I felt more alive than I ever had before. He always made me feel like this. He lowered himself slowly over me and his lips caressed mine. I kissed him, but not fully. I knew he wanted me to, but I wanted it to last – I didn't want to rush. I wanted our lovemaking to be slow. He groaned as if I were teasing him in some way. I wasn't - I was teasing myself, and I enjoyed that. The urge to just let him take me was unbearable because I knew what pleasures lay ahead, but I wanted to hold off for as long as I could. The longer I waited, the better the end when it came.

My heart raced and I think he could sense it. As if he were unable to resist any longer, he buried his hands in my long, dark hair and pushing into me, we kissed at last. His skin felt cold against mine. Entwining our bodies as if we were one, he pinned me to the bed. Arching my back, I let him kiss every part of my face, neck, and breasts. He released a gentle moan, and this just made my heart race faster still.

"I love you, Sophie," he whispered in my ear. Now I could feel his heart racing. He ran his mouth over my neck, and I felt his teeth nip at the skin. His whole body seemed to tense up.

We had made love many times before, but there was an intensity about him tonight that I hadn't felt before. He pressed me flat against the bed and I writhed beneath him. I gasped, but not out of fear. Not yet.

"I want you, Sophie," he groaned. "I want all of you."

"Then take me," I whispered against his chest, and I thought my heart was going to explode.

I felt his whole body shudder, and my back arched again as he moved over me. Then, he twisted as if his spine was stretching out of shape. I opened my eyes a fraction and looked into his face. His jaw looked as if it was locked tight and he gripped the bed sheets with his fists. Throwing my arms around his neck and wrapping my legs about him, I pulled him close; I couldn't fight it anymore.

Then, like crying out in pain, his back made a cracking sound as if every one of his ribs were breaking. He lunged backwards and sat kneeling at the foot of my bed. He threw his head back and I screamed as what looked like a pair of fangs cut their way through his gums. A jet of blood shot out and covered my breasts and face.

He clutched at the air with his hands and I watched in horror as his hands transformed into a set of razor-sharp claws. Smearing his blood from my face, I shook with fright as his ears grew into points. Then, his whole face began to change shape. His nose contorted into something similar to a snout and lengths of wiry, black hair bristled from every part of his naked body. Then there was a sound, like a beating heart – and it was loud and filled the room. It was then that I saw two giant black wings flapping behind him.

It wasn't that I found him hideous; it was the thought that just moments ago I had been making love with this black-haired creature who was now perched at the end of my bed. All I could do was scream and pull the bed clothes up around me. I couldn't believe that it was him, that he had hidden this from me. I felt cheated and betrayed – not scared. Tears ran down my face as I looked at the beautiful creature before me.

"Sophie!" he said, but his voice had changed. It was deeper and had a booming quality.

I didn't know what to think or how to feel. I loved him – more than I had loved anyone before. He had meant everything to me. But he had cheated me – fooled me, and that made me angry. Covering my face with my hands, I sobbed uncontrollably and turned away from him.

"Sophie," he tried again, "You don't have to be scared."

"Get away from me!" I shrieked, kicking out with my feet.

"Sophie, let me explain," his voice boomed. "I love you!"

I peered back at him over the top of the sheet. Part of me wanted to go to him. I loved him, and even as he sat like a giant bat at the end of my bed, a part of me still wanted him. He had a look of brutality about him that I knew had always been there – and that's what had turned me on about him. He wasn't like other guys – he didn't make love to me like other guys had. But to know that I still wanted him now, that I was aroused by this beast, scared me – I felt ashamed and repulsed by myself – not him.

So, staring at him over the top of the blankets, I screamed, "Get away from me! You freak – you animal! Get out!"

"I love -" he begged.

"GET OUT!"

He jumped from the bed, where only moments before we had been making love, and went to the windows. Throwing them open, he climbed onto the ledge. He looked back at me with his dead, black eyes, and to know that I still loved him and always would, broke my heart.

"I'm so sorry," he growled.

Then, leaping from the window, he spread his wings and shot into the night sky. Throwing back the bed covers, I raced to the window and watched him disappear into the night as tears...

...ran down my face. I opened my eyes and brushed them away. Even though I was free from my nightmare, those feelings of love and loss for the creature I had seen were still raw inside of me. It was like I was in love, but I didn't exactly know who with or why. How could I have such intense feelings for someone I had never met, let alone seen? As I swung my legs over the side of the bed, I knew that the creature in my dreams was the letter writer – he was called Potter. I might not have met him – but he was a real and living person – the cop who I'd shot had told me so – and for reasons I didn't understand, I was in love with him.

10

Sophie

I spent the next few weeks hiding out at the farmhouse at the top of the hill. On the morning I had woken from the dream about the man called Potter, I had thrown on my dirty old clothes and made my way back down the narrow coastal path to the small town of Beechers Hope. I knew I was in trouble and by now, most of the police force would be looking for me. The cop who had killed the Skin-walker had probably been discovered on the road by now. The gun that had shot him and the Skin-walker was covered in my prints. They were going to believe him over me any day. Everyone would be ready to believe that I had shot them both in my escape. I had no one to turn to other than my mother and father, and did I really want to drag them into the nightmare that I now found myself in?

I had switched off my mobile phone, removed the battery, and tossed it into a stream minutes after running away from that cop as he bled on the road. I had been around enough police investigations in my role as a pathologist to know that my phone could be traced – even if it was switched off. The battery had to go too. I had enough cash on me to last a week or two, if I was careful – but then what? Credit cards were a big no-no as well. They would leave an electronic footprint every time I used them. I might as well fire a flare into the sky and scream, "come and get me, boys!" But I knew the longer that I hid, the longer I went on the run, the guiltier I looked.

I needed time to come up with a plan. This man Potter was somehow connected, I was sure of that, but all I had was his letters. The young woman, Kiera Hudson, was also a big part, but where was she now? If I could find either of them, then perhaps I could prove my innocence somehow. The blood would have helped me prove to the authorities that something crazy was going on, but that cop had taken the vial.

With my brain working overtime, I reached Beechers Hope. Although the streets were pretty quiet, I was paranoid that everyone I passed would somehow know that I was on the run and call the police. It didn't help that it was mid-January, winter, and the seaside town of Beechers Hope was yet to fill with tourists and holiday makers. That wouldn't happen for months yet. I could have disappeared amongst them and no one would have given me a second look.

With my head bent low, I cut across the town square and disappeared up a narrow side street. Halfway up, I spied a charity shop. In desperate need of some new clothes, and with little cash, I thought it would be an ideal place to find myself something new to wear. I pushed open the door and a bell tinkled above my head. The shop smelt musty, and someone had tried to disguise this by placing small bunches of lavender around the shop in glass vases. There were racks of clothes and shelves with second-hand books. There was also a display case that was full of odd-looking knick-knacks that had been donated to the charity shop.

Along the far wall was a counter and behind it sat an old woman with a fuzz of white hair. Her skin was wrinkled up like an old prune and her puckered lips had been smeared crudely with red lipstick. Hearing the bell ring, the old woman looked up from a book that she was reading. She waved a gnarled looking hand in my direction and then went back to her reading.

I slipped between the racks of clothing, looking for anything halfway decent. The hangers made a jingling noise as I pushed the clothes aside, checking out each garment. I wanted something that would be completely different from the clothes I would normally wear. If I were to stay on the run, I needed to look different than how I usually looked; I needed a new identity somehow. A lot of the clothes on display were more suited for the older woman. Then, as I looked about the shop, something caught my eye. It was a pretty-looking dress that was covered in a faint floral pattern. It wasn't something I would normally have been seen dead in. I took the dress from its hanger and held it against me for size. It looked as if it might fit, but it was more like something a hippie would wear. There was another dress very similar a couple of rows down, so I took that from its hanger, too. Again, it was something a tree-hugger might wear, but it was different from my usual tastes. Folding the dresses over my arm, I knew that I would also need a coat. I found a long brown coat with a fake fur collar – very seventies – and knowing that it would suit the whole new hippie look I was reluctantly going for, I took the items to the counter.

"Do you need a bag?" the old woman asked me as she removed the hand-written price tags from the clothes.

"Yes, please," I mumbled, trying not to make eye contact with her. Then, taking the coat, I added, "I'll put this on now – it's freezing outside."

"Okay, dear," the old woman smiled sweetly at me, and I noticed that some of her red lipstick was stuck to her front teeth. It looked like she had been eating strawberry jam.

I took the coat and put it on. It had a belt that I fastened around my waist.

"It suits you," she smiled again. "Funny time of year to come on holiday."

"Oh, I'm not on holiday," I smiled back. "I'm just passing through."

I gave the old woman the money for the clothes, and taking the bag, I headed out of the store.

"Goodbye, dear," she called out.

Without looking back, I waved my hand in the air. The bell tinkled overhead again as I stepped out into the street. I pulled the fur collar of the coat up about my neck, and it felt warm and soft against my cheeks. I didn't want to hang around in town for too long, so I headed back down the street to a small supermarket that was situated in the town square. I filled a basket with cans of food. I didn't even know if the farm that I was squatting in had an oven or a stove, and if it did, would it even work. But there was a fire, even if I could heat up a few cans of beans, that would be something. I took some milk and bread and anything else that I could think of. As I headed for the cash register, I checked my pockets for my cash, then remembered I was wearing the new coat I had bought from the charity shop. My cash was folded away in the back pocket of my jeans. Then, as I went to take my hand from the coat pocket, I felt something. It was small and square, about the size of a credit card. I pulled it out and realised that it was a driving licence and it must have belonged to whoever had donated the coat to the charity shop. I turned it over it my hands and looked down at the tiny picture of the face that stared back at me. The woman was pretty, about the same age as me, and we could have looked quite similar if it wasn't for the fact that she had light blonde hair and mine was dark brown. Her name was printed beneath her picture and it read *Caroline Hughes*.

Then, with an idea creeping into my mind, I headed back amongst the isles of the supermarket and took a bottle of blonde hair dye from the display and placed it into my basket.

11

Potter

I closed the door to Kiera's flat behind me. After what had happened in the Grandma's flat, I was keen to make sure that this time I had the right place. Being shot and called "kinky" was enough for one night and I just wanted to get back to the manor. Like the other flat had been, Kiera's was also in darkness. This time, I risked having the aid of some light, so I took my cigarette lighter out and flipped it on. A flame of orange light lit the darkness before me. I was standing in a small, tidy room. There were no newspaper cuttings tacked to the wall, and at first I feared I'd gotten the wrong flat again. Why did everything have to be *pushed*? With the light from the flame in my hand, I tiptoed across the room to the window. There was the chair that Kiera had so often described sitting in, and then I saw a picture frame by the window.

Holding the lighter above it, I could see that it was a picture of Kiera and an older-looking man. I could see the likeness. They both had those hazel eyes that lit up Kiera's face and both had jet-black hair. I'd never seen Kiera's father, but I knew that it was him in the picture. Kiera had spoken fondly of her father and had told me how close they had been. She had promised him, before he died of cancer, that she would find her mother for him. She certainly did that. I turned around, and taking the picture with me, I headed towards another door, which led into Kiera's bedroom. In the light from the flame, I saw a rucksack on the floor by a set of drawers. I picked it up and put the picture inside it – Kiera would like to see that photo again. I then opened the drawers. As soon as my fingers felt the soft silk of the underclothes, I knew that I had the right place – there was no doubt this time. Beneath the bras and knickers, my fingers brushed across something similar in shape and size to a wallet. I pulled it out and the silver badge twinkled in the light. I placed it into the rucksack and then I snatched a handful of her underwear. As I was shoving it into the bag someone spoke from within the darkness.

"Who in the hell are you?" the voice asked.

"How does the same shit happen to me twice in one night?" I breathed turning around, half expecting to see another dried up old woman peering at me from the darkness.

But it wasn't an old woman who was staring back at me; it was someone much younger by the sound of their voice. Holding the lighter up, I moved towards whoever it was.

"Stay where you are," the female voice snapped.

"Who are you?" I asked.

"Keep back," the voice came again, and I could sense the fear in it.

"I'm not going to hurt you," I tried to assure her, the flame wavering before me. In the flickering light, I could see that whoever it was standing in the darkness had long, blonde hair. It was thick and curled around her shoulders. I moved closer towards her.

"Keep away from me or I'll scream," she threatened.

"You're not going to scream," I whispered. "You're hiding in here or you would have come out of the shadows already."

I moved closer still and as I did, the female rushed from the corner and tried to get past me. Shooting my arm out, I grabbed her by the wrist and yanked her towards me. Holding the light inches from her face, I looked into her eyes. At first I didn't recognise her, but when I did, I thought my mind was playing tricks on me. Her hair used to be dark brown, but now it was blonde – something else that had been *pushed* perhaps?

Looking into her face, and my heart beginning to race, I whispered, "Sophie, is that really you?"

She yanked her arm free of my grip and staggered backwards. "My name's not Sophie," she said, pulling something from the pocket of the long, brown coat she was wearing. Flashing a small piece of plastic I.D. in front of my face, she snapped, "See, my name's Caroline Hughes. I don't know who Sophie is."

Maybe she wasn't called Sophie now that the world had been pushed – perhaps her name was really Caroline Hughes? I wondered. But then again, her father referred to her as Sophie. But I wouldn't tell her I'd seen him. I didn't want her to think I'd been looking – searching – for her. "You used to be called Sophie once," I said softly, not really knowing if I should have told her that. But I'd said it, it was out there, and I couldn't take it back.

"What's that s'posed to mean?" she mumbled, placing the I.D. back into her pocket.

"Nothing, it doesn't matter," I said, realising that she didn't know me. I shouldn't say any more; Sophie – Caroline – had no idea that the world had been *pushed*. She had been born into a different world where we had never met – were we had never been lovers.

"Are you a cop?" she asked me, inching backwards towards the door.

"Not anymore," I told her, and it felt weird inside to be standing so close to her again and having to pretend that we were strangers.

"What's your name?" she asked me, as she reached the door to the living room.

"Potter," I told her.

Then, before I'd had a chance to react, Sophie shot across the room and kicked me straight in the nuts.

"Jesus!" I groaned. "What was that for?"

"For breaking up me and Marty!" she shouted.

"Who the fuck is Marty?" I said, rubbing my bollocks.

"He was my boyfriend and we broke up because of those letters you sent me. He thought I was sleeping with you."

"You *were* sleeping with me," I tried to remind her.

"I don't ever remember having sex with you!" she shouted.

"You really know how to boost a man's ego," I shot back.

She raised her hand as if to strike me again, and I snatched hold of her fist. "Once is enough, sweetheart."

"I'm not your sweetheart!" she spat. "You're a creep."

"I thought you said you didn't remember me," I said, staring at her.

Then, turning her back on me, she went into the living room. I followed her and watched as she picked up a holdall from the floor. She reached inside and pulled out a bunch of envelopes. Chucking them at me, she said, "These are the letters that you sent me."

They scattered at my feet and I bent down and picked one up. The address on the front was unreadable, smudged beyond recognition, but her name was clear and I could see that it was my handwriting. I opened the letter and read the first few lines. Just reading them stirred the feelings that I'd once had for her within me. I remembered sitting alone in those cheap motel rooms as I had penned those letters to her.

"You wrote them, didn't you?" she asked, her voice sounding calmer now.

"Yes," I said, gathering up the letters and handing them back to her. With a certain amount of reluctance, she snatched them back and placed them into her bag.

"Why?" she asked. "You don't even know me."

Looking at her and not knowing where to start, or even if I should, I said, "I don't know how to explain..."

"You didn't have any difficulty in explaining how you felt for me in those letters," she said.

Sitting down in Kiera's chair by the window, and with the flame from the Zippo lighter flickering in my hand, I said, "We did use to know each other once, but it was a long way away from here."

"Where?" she snapped, placing her hands on her hips.

"I think it's more of a case of *when* rather than *where*," I said, looking at her, and to see her standing there made the feelings that I'd once had for her bubble up inside of me, and I hated myself for feeling like that.

"What's that s'posed to mean?" she quizzed, taking a seat in the armchair opposite me.

"I'm not sure even if I know the answer to that," I told her. "The world has been pushed."

"Pushed, how?"

"It's hard to explain," I stared, "but I first met you a few years ago. You were studying music..."

"I've never studied music," she corrected me. "I'm a pathologist. I studied medicine."

"You didn't have blonde hair, either," I half-smiled at her. "It used to be dark brown."

"I dyed it."

"Oh," I said. "It looks good."

"Cut the bullshit," she said. "Just start explaining to me why you sent those letters."

Looking into her eyes, I could see the reflection from the flame dancing in them and I said, "Before the world got pushed, whether you believe me or not, you did use to study music. I met you at college. I wasn't studying anything really – I was just having a good time. Then, I met you and all that changed."

"How come?"

"I fell in love with you and you fell in love with me," I told her. "But one night I scared you real bad and you told me to leave. So I did. But I couldn't forget you. I loved you, Soph...Caroline. I wrote you those letters trying to explain...hoping that I could win you back."

Staring at me, she said, "So what did you do that scared me so much?"

"This," I said, standing and taking off the scarecrow's coat. I rolled back my shoulders and let my wings unfold. They beat up and down on either side of me. I locked my jaw as my fangs came through and splayed my fingers to release my claws. I looked at her and this time she didn't look scared, just curious.

12

Sophie

To see him standing before me as I had seen him in my dreams – *nightmares* – made my flesh turn cold. Not out of fear, but in realisation that I must have known him before - how else had I dreamt about him? Why else would I have the feelings that I did for him? I felt as if I had once loved this man, but he had died many years ago and I had moved on with my life and fallen in love with another. But he had now returned. He hadn't been dead at all but just lost, and all those feelings that I'd once had for him – which I believed were gone – now came rushing to the front. I felt overwhelmed, but I couldn't show him that. Although I had feelings of love for this man who stood before me, I didn't know him. He was like a perfect stranger to me.

"So you're no longer scared of me?" he asked, his black wings trailing behind him.

"Do I need to be scared of you?" I breathed, unable to take my eyes off him. I remembered the dream in which I had seen him standing in my bedroom as I screamed at him to get out.

He must have sensed something in the tone of my voice or in the way that I stared at him as he looked at me and said, "You do remember, don't you?"

"No," I said, shaking my head. I didn't want to tell him I had dreamt of him. To admit to that would mean I would have to admit to the feelings that I had for him. I couldn't do that. This wasn't real, it wasn't happening to me. I had only ever had one life, the one where I lived with my mum and dad, where I had trained in medicine, where I had fallen in and out of love with a sweet guy called Marty, who was now dead...

"You're lying," Potter said, as he came across the gloomy room towards me.

"I'm not," I said, looking away. I couldn't look into his eyes. "If what you say is true – that the world has somehow been *pushed*, how come I received your letters?"

"I don't know the answer to that," he said, stopping in front of my chair.

I could hear his breathing in the semi-darkness and the humming sound that his wings seemed to make as they beat gently together. I wasn't scared of him, not like I had been in my dreams. I wanted to reach out and hold him, to be close to him, but I was scared that if I did, it would feel like I was holding a perfect stranger.

"You know what I say is true," he said.

"No, I don't," I said back. "It doesn't make sense."

"And that's why I came back to look for you," he said. "I was hoping that you might have some answers."

"I don't have any," I told him, and then added, "Where have you come back from?"

"The dead," he said. "I was murdered – you weren't the only woman who has ripped my heart out. I died and came back." He looked at me. "Why don't you look surprised by that?"

"Do you know someone by the name of Kiera Hudson?" I asked, looking up at him.

"Yes, why?" he asked curiously.

"Because she was murdered too," I told him, my eyes fixed on his. "I was the pathologist carrying out the post-mortem on her, when she came back to life and went running into the night."

"You mean that it was you who..."

"Yes," I cut in. "Two others showed up and..."

"Isidor and Kayla," Potter said.

"Who?"

"My friends," he said. "We've all come back from the dead. But we didn't come back to the world that we once knew. The one where me and you had once been lovers, where U2 was called U2 and London was called London."

"What are you talking about?" I gasped, getting up from the chair and going to the window.

78

"This is not the world that I once knew," he insisted, following me to the window.

"So in this other world you talk about, creatures like you roamed around free did they?" Then looking him up and down, I added, "What are you meant to be anyhow, some kinda vampire?"

"A Vampyrus, actually," he said, sounding a little pissed off. "And besides, we didn't just wander about – people would have stared, don't you think?"

"They don't stare at the wolves," I told him matter-of-factly.

"Wolves?" he said, gripping my arm again.

"You're hurting me," I said, pulling free of him. "The Skin-walkers, they're wolves that steal the skins of humans." Then, looking him up and down again, I added, "Wait until they get a look at you."

"We didn't just stroll about. We lived in secret, unknown to the humans," he hissed. "That's why you were so scared of me, when you saw me like this. In the world before it was *pushed* – creatures like me existed only in books and movies. No one must see me like this – not here."

I looked at him and he stared back at me. Then as if reading my thoughts, he said, "Who have you told about Kiera Hudson?"

"Is she a Vampyrus like you then?" thinking of what Marty had told me about her blood.

"Have you told anyone?" he barked, his eyes turning even darker, if that were possible.

"I gave Marty some of your friend's blood to test," I said sheepishly. "I also told him her name. But that doesn't count, because Marty is..."

"Where is the blood now?" Potter snapped, gripping my arm again.

"A cop took it from me," I started to explain.

"Cop!" Potter growled. "What cop?"

"The one I shot," I said, trying to pull my arm free of his claws.

"You shot a cop?" he asked, raising an eyebrow. "You really have been *pushed*."

"He made me shoot him," I told him, squirming free. "And he knew all about you."

"What did he know?" Potter snapped at me.

"How should I know?" I said. "But I don't think he liked you very much. He said you were a wise arse."

"Did you tell him about Kiera?" he asked me, his voice sounding anxious.

"He wanted to know about the girl who had come back to life in the morgue, so I told him her name," I said.

"You did what?"

"He made me!" I shouted at him, feeling pissed off that I was getting the blame for all of this. "He already knew about her and the blood – he just didn't know her name that was all."

"Who else have you told about Kiera?" he breathed, his fangs just inches from my face.

"Just Marty and the cop," I said. "But Marty's dead now..."

"Shhh!" he hissed, covering my mouth with one of his giant claws.

Then, from outside I could hear the sound of vehicles screeching to a halt outside. With his free hand, Potter opened the curtains just an inch and a spray of pulsating blue light lit up the room.

"Cops!" he groaned.

Pushing his hand away from my mouth, I peered through the gap in the curtains. "There is another thing I haven't mentioned; most of the police force is currently searching for me."

"I don't think they're after you," Potter said, staring down at the mass of cops below and at an ancient old woman wearing a nightgown.

"Why would the police be after you?" I asked him.

Then, as if in answer to my question, I saw the little old lady point up at the window and shriek, "That's the pervert I caught sniffing my knickers!"

"You did what?" I gasped, stepping away from him.

"I'm not a pervert!" Potter barked at me.

"Well there's about five or six coppers down there who think you are," I said.

"And they're not going to catch me without a fight," Potter growled, spreading his wings.

13

Potter

"Empty your bag!" I shouted over the thumping sound of the cops charging up the stairs towards the flat.

"Why?" Sophie – Caroline – said back.

"Just do it!" I snapped.

She pulled the letters, some clothing, and an iPod from her holdall. Holding out the rucksack towards her, I said, "Put the stuff in here."

"Why?" she asked again.

"Because I need you to carry the rucksack. I can't, remember?" I said, beating the wings that hung from my back.

"Oh, yeah," she said, understanding the point that I was trying to make.

"Have you got any money?" I asked, as the cops started to pound on the door.

"Not much," she said, stuffing the rucksack with her belongings and my scarecrow coat. "Why do we need money?"

"If we're going on the run, we'll need some," I said, racing into the kitchen.

I knew that humans often hid cash at home, usually in a cookie jar or something similar. When I'd been masquerading as a cop, I'd been to many burglaries where money had been stolen from such a place. I threw open Kiera's kitchen cupboards, as one of the coppers started to order from outside that I open the door before they smashed it down. I pulled cups and plates from the cupboard and there, sitting at the back, was a small jar with "Cookies" written across the front. I ripped off the lid and tipped out the contents.

"Bingo!" I shouted, seeing a roll of notes spill onto the kitchen counter. I snatched them up, put them into my jeans pocket, and raced back into the living room.

Sophie threw the rucksack over her back and looking at me, she said "What now?"

"We fight," I said, flashing my fangs and claws at her.

"But I thought you said no one should see you like this," she reminded me.

"Don't worry, they won't be around long enough to tell anyone about me," I said. "Now get behind me!"

No sooner had Sophie ducked behind my wings, the door to Kiera's flat came crashing in. With my claws up and wings spread, I leapt towards the coppers who came pouring through the doorway. Whoever or whatever they had been expecting - it wasn't me - and I saw the fear in their eyes for just a moment before I removed two of their heads with one quick swipe of my claws. The *thump-thump* sound of their heads bouncing away down the stairs meant nothing to me, but the coppers who watched them roll away began to scream. Bursting onto the landing, I pin-wheeled my arms and opened up the belly of the nearest copper. There was a plopping sound as his intestines burst out of him and spilt onto the landing. The cop looked at me, his eyes wide and mouth open as if he wasn't quite sure of what had just happened to him. Then, realising that his guts were slipping out of him, he started to gather them up in his hands. I watched as the red and pink lengths of intestines slipped through his fingers like oily lengths of rope. He then staggered forward, his feet becoming entangled in his own guts, and he went sprawling down the stairs.

Although the final copper was screaming, I realised that he wasn't screaming in fear, but in anger. I looked at him and could see his eyes were burning a hot white-yellowy colour. The last time I had seen eyes like that was when I was staring into the face of a Lycanthrope. Before I'd the chance to react, the Skin-walker bounded towards me, shoving me back across the room. Sophie spun away from me and landed in the chair by the window. From the corner of my eye, I saw the chair upturn, taking Sophie with it. The wolf came at me again, and as it did, it began to change.

Its face almost seemed to rip apart as a long, brown snout shot out. Its shoulders and neck grew, the buttons from its shirt spraying away. The copper's hands tripled in size and began to turn in to giant paws as it lunged at me. The paws struck me in the chest and sent me flying backwards through the window in a shower of glass. I spun towards the ground, my wings covered in shards of razor-sharp glass and splinters of wood from the window frame.

The roof of the police car crumpled like a sheet of tissue paper as I crashed into it. There was a groaning sound from inside. The car door flew open and another cop staggered out. I shook the glass from me, and slid down the windscreen and stood on the bonnet. From above me, I could hear Sophie start to scream. Launching myself into the air, I shot upwards and back through the broken window.

The Skin-walker was clawing at Sophie as she cowered beneath the chair. Its shirt had completely fallen away now, and its back was a mass of muscle which was covered in shiny brown fur. The wolf howled and barked as Sophie scuttled away on her back like a giant crab. Jumping from the window, I landed on the wolf's back and slid my claws into its huge neck. It spun around, whipping its tail, desperate to throw me off. I held fast, digging my claws deeper and deeper into its throat. The wolf's blood felt hot and tacky as it poured over my claws. I sliced my fingers back and forth, until I felt the wolf's head come away from its hulking shoulders. It slumped forward and then rolled onto its side. I flew backwards, snatching Sophie into my arms. Before flying back out of the window, I looked back to see that the dead wolf once again looked like a human as it lay decapitated in the middle of Kiera's living room.

No sooner had I swooped from the window with Sophie in my arms, the sound of gun fire boomed from below, as bullets went whizzing past me. Sophie clung to me, and I looked down to see that she had her head pressed against my chest, with her eyes shut tight. Spinning through the night, I perched on the roof of a nearby house.

Setting Sophie down, I said, "Hold on, I'll be back in a moment or two."

"You're joking me," she squealed, griping the roof with her fingernails.

Back-flipping off the roof, I circled in the air and spied the last of the coppers. He was shielding himself behind the damaged police car and firing wildly up at me. Rolling back my shoulders, I sped towards the ground, cutting through the air like an arrow. I was on him so fast that he was still pulling the trigger on the gun as I swept back up into the night with his head hanging from between my jaws. I looked back to see his headless corpse twitch then wobble as it collapsed onto the ground. I spat his head away, and span around in the air. It was as I banked right in the direction of Sophie on the roof that I saw the old woman, who was convinced that I was a pervert, standing in the street below. She was screaming. Knowing that I couldn't leave any witnesses alive, I flew down towards her.

I landed on the pavement as she threw her hands up as if to protect herself from me. I walked towards her. Gently, I took her hands in mine, and I knew I couldn't kill her. I didn't want to kill her. Leaning in close, I could feel her trembling.

Then, placing my mouth next to her ancient ear, I whispered, "You can't tell anyone what you saw here tonight. Because if you do, I'll come and strangle you with those pretty knickers of yours."

I felt her head nod next to mine, as she stifled her sobs.

"Do we have an agreement?" I asked.

"Okay," she said, her voice steadying.

Pulling away from her and wondering what kind of life she had lived alongside these Skin-walkers, I said, "There's a beautiful world out there – I've seen it – and me and my friends will *push* it back for you, I promise."

Then I was gone, soaring back up to the rooftop where Sophie was now hanging by her fingernails. As I raced towards her, Sophie lost her grip and began to plummet back towards the ground. Just feet from the pavement, I snatched her back into my arms and rocketed up into the night.

"You arsehole!" she screeched, pounding her fists against my naked chest. "You could've killed me!"

"And here I was thinking I just saved your life," I half-grinned at her.

"That copper was right about you," she shouted over the sound of the roaring wind. "You are a wise arse!"

"And that's why you fell in love with me," I said, racing into the clouds with her.

14

Sophie

I thought the copper who had killed the happy-zapper in the police car had been violent, but the way Potter had killed those police officers back at the flat was something else. It had been like watching a wild animal. He had moved with such speed, agility, and skill – if that's what you could call it. He hadn't shown any reluctance in killing any of them and somehow I got the impression that he was enjoying himself – like a lion hunting down a zebra. The animal does it out of instinct – it knows nothing else – and that's what watching Potter had been like. But unlike in my dreams, he hadn't scared me. If there had been another Sophie in a world that hadn't been *pushed,* as Potter had described it, then I was different now. Maybe because I had grown up in a world with monsters, and I was no longer scared of the one who held me in his arms as we raced through the night sky.

Clouds raced past us and every so often, if I dared to look down, I could see the fields racing away far below, bathed in the silver light of the moon. He sped up and there was a rumbling sound like thunder. I stared up at Potter's face, and it looked as hard as stone. His eyes were dark, and his skin pale like marble.

"Where are you taking me?" I shouted over the sound of the rushing wind.

"I was hoping you might know somewhere," he said, without looking down at me.

"There's a farmhouse that I've been hiding out in," I yelled. "It's pretty secluded. We could hide out there for a few days."

"I haven't got a few days," he said, and to hear that made me feel alone again. But was that really how I felt? Wasn't I just a little bit disappointed that he would be leaving me so soon?

"Where is this farmhouse?" he asked me.

"On a hill near a town called Beechers Hope," I said. "Do you know where that is?"

Without answering me, Potter banked sharply to the left, and my stomach did that somersault thing that happens when you take off in an aeroplane. What had taken me a week by foot and the odd bus journey to travel, Potter covered the distance between Havensfield to Beechers Hope in about half an hour. With his eyes fixed firmly ahead, we shot through the clouds and circled high above the town of Beechers Hope.

"Where's the farmhouse?" he asked in my ear.

In the distance I could see the black silhouette of the hill against the night sky. I pointed at it and said, "Over there."

Potter covered the last half of a mile in what seemed like seconds, and it wasn't long before he was setting me on my feet again outside the derelict farmhouse. With a shrug of his shoulders, I watched in wonder as his wings seemed to shrink away into his back. He clenched his fists and locked his jaw as his claws and fangs disappeared. He wrenched the rucksack from my back and pulled out the filthy-looking coat he had been wearing. Potter put it on and pushed open the broken down front door.

"I thought you said you had to go," I reminded him.

Looking back at me, he said, "I've got a couple of things I want to ask you first."

"Oh yeah," I said. "Like what?"

"Like, what you were doing at Kiera's flat tonight?"

Potter lit the fire, and pulling up two battered armchairs, we sat before the roaring flames. The light from the fire cast away that pale look his skin had, and gave his face and chest a warm glow. He held his hands before the fire and rubbed them together and I could see that they were still streaked with blood from the cops he had killed at the flat.

"So how come you were at Kiera's flat?" he asked me.

"My life hasn't been the same since she woke up that night in the morgue," I started to explain. "When the police arrived, I stole the sample of blood that I had taken from her for DNA analysis. I didn't want the cops to have it."

"Why not?" he asked me.

"It's not every day that a corpse you're working on suddenly sits up and strolls out of the lab," I told him. "I hoped that her blood would hold the answers. So instead of following the cop back to the police station to give my statement, I gave him the slip and went to Marty's. He worked in a lab that did work on the human genes. I knew that if anyone could find out what this Kiera Hudson was all about, then he could."

"And what did he find out?" he asked me, moving to the edge of the armchair.

"That her blood wasn't strictly human," I said, looking him straight in the eyes. "He said that her blood wasn't too dissimilar to that of a vampire bat. He told me to look after the blood and not to tell anyone about it."

"And that was it?" he pushed.

"I think so, but it's like things became muddled after that," I said thoughtfully.

"Muddled?"

"Marty and I had been separated for over six months, he had met someone else," I told him, and part of me, on a subconscious level, wanted to let him know that I was single. "I thought of him as a friend, that was all. But I think he tried to seduce me or something, because I remember him laying me down onto his bed and kissing me. It was then that he asked me what had been the girl's name that the sample of blood had come from, so I told him. I must have fallen asleep, because the next thing I can remember is waking up on his bed and hearing him shouting in the street outside. It was then that he was hit by the car."

Potter sat quietly as I explained what had happened when the happy-zapper cop had turned up. I told him how he had driven me out into the country and the other cop had killed him. I went on to explain how I fled. I didn't know what to do or where to run. I knew that I couldn't go back to my parents' house, as that would have been the first place that the cops would look for me.

"My parents are getting on now," I said, and to think of them hurt me. "I haven't had any contact with them for weeks, and I miss Archie."

"Archie?" Potter asked, cocking an eyebrow at me.

"My dog," I told him, and an odd look came over his face. "Are you okay?"

"Yeah, fine," he nodded.

So I started to tell Potter how, by accident more than anything, I had ended up in Beechers Hope and at the farm. "I knew that I couldn't just keep aimlessly wandering the countryside," I said. "I needed to start making plans. I went into town to buy some supplies and new clothes and it was while I was there that I found this in the coat that I bought." Then, fishing the driving licence out of my pocket, I handed it to him.

Potter leant forward in his chair and studied the plastic I.D. in the light of the fire. "It's a good likeness, but that isn't you, is it?"

I shook my head. "When I saw it, I thought that I could become her, you know, dye my hair, and if I did ever get stopped by the cops, I could flash that and they would believe that I was her – Caroline Hughes."

"So what were you doing in Kiera's flat tonight?" Potter asked again, handing me back the I.D.

"Once I had dyed my hair, put on my new clothes and got used to the idea of being Caroline Hughes, I got more daring, and over the next few days I left the farmhouse and took some walks along the coastal paths. I needed to get my head together and decide exactly what I was going to do. I couldn't pretend that I was Caroline forever. The sea air cleared my head and the quietness of the place helped me focus. I hardly ever saw anyone on my walks, except for this girl and boy I would occasionally see. They seemed to be very much in love as they were always looking into each other's eyes and holding hands. I let them be, as they obviously wanted to be left alone as much as I did.

"I knew that your friend, Kiera Hudson was the key to this somehow, so I thought that perhaps if I could find out who she was, where she lived and so on, I could start to figure out what was happening. Remembering that I had seen a library in the town square, it took me another week or so to pluck up the courage to venture into town in my disguise. When I did, I dressed in the coat that I had bought, pulled the fur collar up about my face, and made sure that I had Caroline Hughes's I.D. with me, just in case I got stopped.

"I never did got stopped. I made my way in and of town without so much as a stare. In the library I paid for half an hour's Internet access and searched for your friend on 192.com. There were three other women listed with that name. I wrote down their home addresses and telephone numbers, which were on the website. One of them was way too old to be your friend and the second had since emigrated. That only left one. I called her number from a public phone box. After several rings, her answer phone cut in and I recognised her voice from when she had spoken to me as she fled the morgue. Over the next few days, I rang that number again several times and each time there was no response, just the message left on her answer phone. Each time I listened to it, the more I became convinced that I had the right Kiera Hudson. But, I knew that I could only be sure if I went to her flat and checked it out for myself.

"So I packed up my things, and running out of cash before leaving Beechers Hope, I withdrew some money from a cash machine. I know I shouldn't have done it, because if anyone was checking my bank records they would know where I was, but as I was leaving the town, I guessed it wouldn't matter," I told him.

"What did you find at the flat?" he asked me.

"Not much," I said. "I'd only been there long enough to check out a picture that was by the window when you showed up. But as soon as I saw that picture, I recognised her and knew that I had found the right Kiera Hudson."

"So what are you going to do now?" he asked me.

I didn't know what I was going to do, if I were to be honest. I hoped that by going to Kiera's flat I would find something, although I wasn't exactly sure what, and prove my innocence in some way. "I could come with you," I suggested, lowering my eyes so I didn't have to look at him.

"Impossible," Potter said.

To hear him dismiss my idea so quickly hurt me, but also made me angry. "You can't just leave me, Potter," I said, staring at him. "What am I meant to do?"

"Hide," he said, and now it was he who looked away from me and into the fire.

"Hide!" I snapped. "What sort of plan is that? What, you're seriously suggesting that I spend the rest of my life pretending to be somebody else?"

"So what where you planning on doing?" he grunted, taking a cigarette from his trouser pocket and lighting it.

"Not ripping the fucking heads off of several cops, that's for sure!" I shouted. "So you just walk back into my life, cause a massacre, and then disappear again? You know, it isn't going to take a freaking genius to work out that those cops were killed by something other than a human." "I never walked back into your life," Potter said, blowing smoke into the air. "You walked into mine."

"You said that you came looking for me," I reminded him.

"Yeah, well maybe I shouldn't have," he snapped. "I made a mistake, okay?"

"No, it's not okay!" I hissed, standing up. "You can't just walk back into my life, stir up old feelings, then disappear again!"

"What old feelings?" he asked, looking up at me as I stood before the fire. "You said you didn't remember me."

Clenching my fists, I shouted, "Why don't you just piss off, Potter!"

Without looking back at him, I stomped up the stairs. I went to the room with the pink coloured bedding, closed the door, lit a candle, and threw myself onto the bed. I just wanted to scream, but I didn't want him to hear it, so I placed a pillow over my head. I felt lost, confused, and angry. I was angrier at myself than Potter – I hated the feelings that I had for him. But hadn't they always been there, hidden just beneath the surface? Potter said before the world had been *pushed* we had been lovers. Maybe somehow those feelings – just like the letters – had seeped across time, through a tear in the fabric of reality and come back to haunt me.

However hard I tried, I couldn't help but feel love for the obnoxious prick who sat downstairs before the fire. I didn't doubt what Potter had told me. I knew in my heart that we had once shared some kind of life together. As I lay on my front, my head buried beneath the pillow, I remembered how sometimes, when Marty was smoking a cigarette, he had reminded me of someone else and that someone else had been Potter. It was like he had been seeping through into my life for as long as I could remember. Maybe I hadn't wanted to remember him – but now that he was back, I just couldn't forget.

I'd heard a story once about a young woman who'd had an accident and had been in a coma for five years or more. When she finally woke, her fiancé had moved on and married someone else – but she had woken feeling the same for him, just as she had when she had slipped into that coma. At the time I had thought how awful that must have been for her – and now I really understood the pain she must have felt. I wanted to go with him. I didn't want to be left alone. I'd been scared of him once – but I was different then. I didn't want to think about him anymore, I just wanted to go to sleep. So swinging my legs over the edge of the bed and standing in the centre of the room, I slipped off my tree-hugger dress and my underwear. Then, as I stood naked, the door to my room swung slowly open and Potter stepped inside.

15

Potter

I sat before the fire and listened to the sound of Sophie's feet marching up the stairs, followed by the slam of a door. With smoke lingering around the tips of my fingers, I brought the cigarette up to my lips and inhaled deeply. The cravings for the red stuff were bad tonight and I knew that I would have to get back to Hallowed Manor soon. The nicotine masked it, but not enough – not tonight.

Why had I come looking for Sophie? I told myself that it was to try and find out what had happened to the world while we had been away – but I knew that was bullshit. Sophie had been *pushed* too – so she wouldn't have known any difference to the life that she was now living. But, she had remembered me. Why and how? And why had those letters turned up? I had sent them from another place, another time, where my heart had been crushed by her. Like I said, it wasn't so much as another *where* – it was another *when*.

I took another cigarette from the pack and lit it, as I thought of how finding Sophie again had brought back some of my own feelings that I had for her. Was that bad? Was I wrong for having those feelings as I had Kiera in my life now? With the cigarette dangling from the corner of my mouth, I couldn't help but remember how much I'd loved Sophie. I could feel the pain again as she screamed at me, telling me to get out. The pain felt real, all over again. I could see myself wandering aimlessly for weeks, from one town to another, writing her those letters, hoping that she would accept me for who and what I really was. Had I been stupid to send those letters? No, I'd been naive and in love. But, then, hadn't Sophie? Hadn't her reaction to me been normal? Christ, what had I expected her reaction to be on seeing a giant bat perching on the end of her bed? And I'd been a numb-nuts coming back to look for her. I'd used her. Whatever had happened between us, Sophie deserved better than that.

I flicked the end of my cigarette into the fire and got up. Taking off my coat, I made my way up the stairs to her room. At the end of the landing, I paused outside her door. Not knowing if again I was doing the right thing or not, I pushed it open and stepped into her room.

She stood in the centre of the room, and she was naked. I half expected her to cover her breasts with her arms and yell at me to get out, but she didn't, she just stood there, her arms by her sides and looked at me.

"What do you want?" she asked me.

"Do you want me to leave?" I said.

"No," she whispered, and the room flickered with candlelight. "Do you want to leave?"

"No," I said, closing the door behind me.

I turned to face her again, and I couldn't help but think of how beautiful she looked in the soft glow of the candlelight. Her long, blond hair flowed over her shoulders and settled against her breasts. Sophie came towards me, and as she did, I felt a thumping sensation race through my body. It was like a ghost of a heart, racing inside of me.

She stopped before me, and we were so close that I could see she was trembling. "I do remember you," she whispered. "I remember everything. I remember how much I loved you and I know how much I hurt you."

"How do you know?" I whispered back.

"The letters you sent me," she said, her eyes looking into mine. "They were full of pain."

"I'm not hurting anymore," I said.

"Are you sure?" she asked as she folded her arms about me. She pulled me so close that I could feel her breasts, soft against my chest and her breath, warm against my cheek.

"I'm sure," I said, closing my eyes. "I'm in love with another."

Sophie seemed to flinch in my arms and pull slightly away from me. "Kiera Hudson?" she asked.

"Yes," I told her. "I love her more than anything."

"But you loved me," she frowned.

I opened my eyes to see that she was staring into them again, and the hurt that I could see there was almost unbearable.

"That was a long time ago, in another *where* and another *when*," I told her.

"What about what we shared," she smiled, pulling me close again. "What about us?"

Gently easing her away from me, I said, "There is no *us* anymore, Sophie; I was wrong to have come back to look for you."

"You came back for me because deep down you still love me," she tried to convince me.

"I came back because I wanted to know what had happened to the world," I explained, not wanting to hurt her feelings, but knowing that I had to be honest with her. "I had no one else."

"You don't mean that," she said, but I could tell by the tears that were standing in her eyes that she knew I was telling her the truth.

"I'm sorry," I shrugged.

"You can't just come back and open up old wounds then disappear again," she whispered, a tear slipping down her cheek. "You might have had time for your feelings to have changed, but to me it seems like only moments ago that we were making love in my room."

"So why didn't you answer my letters?" I snapped.

"I was a child back then," she cried. "I was scared, Potter, but not of you."

"Of what then?"

"Me," she said. "I was scared at how much I wanted you, even though I knew you were a -"

"Monster?" I cut in. "Is that the word you were searching for?"

"Yes," she said, and looked away. "How could I have been in love with a monster? What sort of life would that have been for me?"

"Kiera loves me, even though I am a monster," I told her.

"It's easy for her," she said. "She's a monster too."

"Kiera fell in love with me before she knew what she was," I told her. "She knew I was a monster long before she knew what *she* truly was. Yet, she accepted me for who and what I was. Kiera loves me for everything that I am, for my foul mouth, my chain-smoking, my bad attitude, and violence. Kiera is freaking awesome. There is no one like her."

"She is very beautiful," Sophie mused.

"You just don't get it, do you?" I said, looking at her.

"Get what?"

"It doesn't matter to me how beautiful Kiera looks," I tried to explain. "I couldn't give a monkey's toss if she looked like the Elephant Man and had an arse the size of King Kong – although she does have the sweetest cheeks I've ever seen. But that means nothing to me – it's what Kiera stands for – that's why I'm so in love with her."

"So what does she stand for?" Sophie asked, and I couldn't help but notice the slightest hint of resentment in her voice.

"She has this really annoying habit of wanting to do the right thing the whole time," I said, smiling inside as I thought of her. "She wants to do the right thing by everyone, even if it means that she loses out somehow. She threw herself into the arms of a serial killer because she couldn't bear the thought of others suffering. Kiera is the smartest, bravest, and most selfless person I have ever known. But deep inside, she is so gentle and kind, and sometimes I think that I'm not even good enough to hold her hand, let alone share a life with her."

"She sounds truly amazing," Sophie shrugged, pulling away from me. I watched her take a blanket from the bed and wrap it about her shoulders.

"She is more than amazing," I whispered. "I've never been very good with words or explaining how I feel, but Kiera makes me feel whole and although we're together, she makes me feel free – that's the only way I can describe it."

Brushing the tears from her face, Sophie looked at me. Then, silently she came towards me again, and kissing me softly on the cheek, she said, "Maybe in another *where* or *when,* things might be different between us, but I'm glad that you are happy now and I'm truly sorry that I hurt you the way I did."

"That's done with now," I told her, heading for the door.

"Don't go," she said softly. "Stay with me tonight. We are miles from anywhere, no one will ever know."

"I'll know," I glared, leaving her alone in the room and closing the door behind me.

16

Sophie

I wrapped the blanket around me and rolled onto my side. I felt hurt and humiliated. Why had I asked him to stay the night? I'd just given him another opportunity to knock me back. Maybe that's why he had said no, he wanted me to know how it felt to be hurt, just like I'd hurt him. I couldn't believe that he didn't feel anything for me anymore. I only had to read those letters to know how much he had felt for me. But there was that word again – "had!" Those letters had been sent from another place, another time – from a world that hadn't been pushed. Potter had had a chance to overcome the hurt that I had caused him – whereas, the feelings that I had for him were still fresh and very real.

He made Kiera Hudson sound wonderful and if all the things he had said about her were true, then she was really special. But wasn't I? Potter had been in love with me once, but I had been special to him, too. I closed my eyes and I could see him making love to me and I tried to push those images from my mind. To see them over and over again was torturing me. To know that he was now making love to Kiera like he once made love to me was enough to drive me insane. Why had this happened to me? Why couldn't I have been left to my life, the one with Marty? We had been happy until those letters had shown up on the doormat. I only had feelings for Marty back then, now I felt nothing for him and even though this sounds nasty, I felt it difficult to feel anguish at his death. Did that make me a complete and utter bitch? I didn't want to be. But somehow, my feelings had changed. I no longer felt like the Sophie I had known all my life, I felt like the Sophie that Potter described from his world – the one before it had been pushed.

With the blankets pulled up under my chin and the sound of the icy wind screaming around the eaves, I wondered if there was anyone else out there who was falling asleep tonight next to their husband or wife, suddenly releasing it wasn't them they loved but someone else, a shadowy figure from another *where* and another *when*. Then, as sleep began to take me, I heard the sound of the bedroom door creak open. I didn't move, not an inch. Had Potter changed his mind? Had he been unable to mask his true feelings for me and decided to spend the night with me after all? Just one night. Us together how we used to be, making love until dawn broke, when we would collapse into each other's arms and drift into a peaceful and deep sleep. All I wanted was one night, before he went back to his life with Kiera Hudson.

I heard his feet on the wooden floorboards as he came towards the bed. I kept my eyes closed. My heart began to race as I felt his strong hand fall against my shoulder.

"Sophie," he whispered in my ear. "Sophie, wake up."

Opening my eyes, I rolled over and looked into his dark eyes.

I opened my mouth to speak, but he placed one of his hands against my lips.

"Shhh!" he whispered. "I can hear someone snooping around outside."

At first my heart sank on realising that he hadn't come back to my room for the night, then it sped up when I realised what he had just told me.

"Who..." I started.

"Shhh!" he warned me again, his eyes wide. "Put your clothes on and be quick about it."

Trying to be as quiet as possible, I climbed off the bed and put on my clothes. Potter went to the window and spied through a gap in the curtains.

Once dressed, I went over to him and tried to peek over his shoulder. "Keep back," he hushed.

"Who's out there?" I whispered.

"I don't know. I haven't had a good view of him yet."

"It might be the wind," I said.

"It's not the wind," he hissed. "I saw his shadow, a big shadow."

"A Skin-walker?" I gasped.

"There's only one way to find out," Potter said, snuffing out the candle so that we were in total darkness. I felt his hand slip around mine as he led me from the room and down the stairs. There was a banging sound, and I could see the pale light of the moonlight spilling into the living room from the front door, as it swung open on its hinges.

"Someone's in here," I whispered.

"Shhh!" Potter said again, as I felt his wings unravel from his back and brush against me.

At the bottom of the stairs, Potter let go of my hand and I saw his claws and fangs glisten in the moonlight. The fire had died down a little, but the wind that now howled across the living room sent sparks flying up the chimney.

I could hear my heart beating in my ears as Potter led me from the bottom of the stairs and towards the door. The fire cast long, eerie shadows up the walls. Then, from the corner of my eye, I saw one of the shadows move with such speed that before I'd the chance to scream, Potter was flying backwards across the room. Someone or something was on Potter. In the glow of the fire, I watched Potter stagger to his feet. Then, the shadow that had attacked him appeared from behind the upturned armchair. But it wasn't a shadow, it was a man and I recognised him.

"Potter!" I screamed. "That's the copper who made me shoot him on the road!"

17

Potter

Although I was dead, to look at him made me wonder if I wasn't seeing a ghost.

"Don't just stand there with that stupid look on your face, Potter. We're in serious fucking trouble here!" he said.

"Do you two know each other?" Sophie breathed in disbelief.

I glanced at Sophie, then back at the figure who had appeared from behind the chair. "I don't believe it," I said, struggling to form the words in my mouth.

"What don't you believe, Potter? That you look like a fucking retard standing there with your mouth wide open, or we're in the shit again?" he growled, going to the window and peering out into the dark as if looking for someone.

"But..." I stammered.

"No buts, Potter," he snapped raising his forefinger at me. "Stop standing there with your thumb up your arse and help me block up the doors and windows."

"Who is he?" Sophie whispered at me, watching him pick up the armchair and place it in front of the window.

Ignoring her, I looked back at him and said, "But Murphy, you're dead."

"Yeah and so are you," he shouted. "Now give me a hand here!"

"But..." I started again.

"But what?" he growled.

"You're still wearing those shitty old carpet slippers," I said in wonder, as he stood before me in a crisp-looking police uniform.

"I might be dead," he half-smiled, "but those police boots still play havoc with my corns. Just can't wear the damn things – they hurt like a bitch."

Then, as he hurried across the room towards the other armchair, I noticed for the first time that he was limping again. "You still have the limp," I gasped, remembering how he had been shot by that shithead, Harker all those years ago.

"I didn't until she shot me in the leg," he grunted, eyeing Sophie who stood at the foot of the stairs staring at us.

"You forced me to shoot you!" Sophie snapped at him.

"I was hoping for a small flesh wound," he barked at her. "I wasn't planning on you blowing half my fucking leg off!"

Ignoring him, Sophie shook her head as if waking from a dream, looked at me, and said, "Who is this guy?"

"He's my old sergeant," I told her, still unable to comprehend that he was back.

"Not so much of the old," Murphy grunted as he carried the chair towards the other window. "I'm forty. Might have gone grey early, but that was your fault."

"My fault?" I said, going to help him as he limped across the room with the chair.

"What, with all your moaning and bitching the whole time, Potter," he huffed as he wedged the chair into the window frame, "no wonder I went grey – I'm surprised it didn't all bloody fall out!"

"I never used to moan..." I started.

"You're moaning now," he sighed at me. Then, standing back as if to get a good look at me, he said, "My God, death hasn't changed you, has it? You're still a scruffy-looking arsehole."

"I'm not scruffy-looking," I said.

"Don't argue with your sergeant, Potter," he barked. "Now help me secure this place before they get here."

"Before who gets here?"

"The wolves," he said with a grim look on his face.

"So where's our backup?" I shot back.

"You're looking at it," he half-smiled.

"Things don't change, do they?" I smiled back at him.

Then, from across the room, Sophie shouted, "Can someone *please* tell me what is going on here!"

103

Wheeling around, Murphy limped towards her, and jabbing his finger in the air, he barked, "I'll tell you what's going on here, pretty lady. You used your freaking credit card, that's what's going on!"

"I needed some -" she started, but Murphy didn't give her a chance to finish.

"I killed that filthy Skin-walker for you, took a bullet for you, and all you had to do was disappear for a while and keep your head down," he said, pulling his pipe from his trouser pocket. "But oh no, you had to go on a shopping spree and use your credit card, telling the whole goddamn world where you were!"

"You took a bullet for me?" Sophie gasped. "You set me up to make it look like I'd escaped from you, killed that wolf-thing with the zapper, then I shot you. I'm not surprised the whole world is looking for me."

"I did it to save your life," he shouted gruffly at her, plumes of thick, grey smoke spilling out of his pipe, which dangled from the corner of his mouth.

"Save my life?" Sophie said, sounding as if she were choking. "Well you have a funny way of showing it."

"You signed your own death warrant the night you stole that blood from the morgue," Murphy told her. "Didn't you think it would look just the slightest bit suspicious that a bottle of blood goes missing from a corpse that has just sat up in your morgue? And giving that cop the slip was another stupid idea. Then, you get your ex-boyfriend to carryout tests on that blood – well that was just ridiculous!"

"Who are you calling ridiculous?" Sophie spat. "Look at you - standing there with your bushy silver hair and eyebrows, police uniform, pipe, and carpet slippers – you look like somebody's grandfather who hasn't grown out of playing cops and robbers."

"I'm not a granddad!" Murphy barked. "I'm only forty!"

"You could've fooled me," Sophie yelled back.

"Listen here," Murphy said, pointing the tip of his pipe at her, "I had everything under control until you poked your nose in. I've been back from the dead only months, and in that time I've managed to work my way back into the police – into a position where I could find out what the hell is going on around here – into a position where I would be able to help my friends when they came back."

"Help us with what?" I cut in.

"Push the world back to how it was," Murphy said, staring at me through a thick cloud of pipe smoke.

"Can we do that?" I asked.

"I don't know yet," he said. "I'm still trying to figure it out. But your friend over here has gone and messed things up."

"I messed things up?" Sophie gasped. "What about you? You smashed that cop's head in!"

"I had to get the blood back. If he had found that on you – then the Skin-walkers might have figured out what Kiera truly is and that would have led them back to us."

"And what's so bad about that?" she sneered. Then, looking at me she added, "It's not as if you're going around trying not to draw attention to yourselves. Ripping the heads off Walkers every five minutes isn't going to go unnoticed, you know."

"I was trying to save you," I told her.

"Yeah, well maybe I don't want to be saved by you and your friend anymore," she said, glancing at me, then at Murphy. "Maybe I should tell the Skin-walkers what you really did out on the road, tell them about the blood..."

"Tell them what you like," Murphy shouted. "They won't believe you. I've destroyed Kiera's blood sample – it doesn't exist anymore, but the gun with your prints all over it does."

"You bastard," she hissed at him.

"Not a bastard, a friend," he said. "But you just don't see it. That animal was going to hurt you real bad if I hadn't have killed him on that road. I had to make it look like you'd escaped so my position wasn't compromised. I did what I did because I didn't have a choice. If you hadn't have taken that blood, then you would never have been involved in this. In fact, I was on the verge of convincing them that you must be dead. I told them that you were very badly injured in the car crash. As it had been some weeks and you hadn't been sighted, I'd almost got them to believe that you were lying injured in a ditch somewhere and that you must have frozen to death in the cold. Then you go and use your credit card, and they start hunting for you all over again."

"But why?" Sophie said. "I stole some blood – big deal."

"The wolves have been waiting for hundreds of years for an angel to come," Murphy explained, as he sucked on his pipe. "All they know is that this angel will be female and will be aided by four others. They believe that she will come and destroy the Treaty that exists between them and the humans and will eventually destroy the wolves. They don't know her name or when she will come. All they know is that this angel will be dead already. So, when they heard that a female corpse had come back to life in your morgue, they...well, let's just say they were just a tiny bit curious. There was that cop with the broken legs and the lab assistant who both kept babbling on about the young woman who came back to life. I didn't know how much they knew or what they had seen, but before I'd managed to speak with them, they had both died."

"Yeah, one died of having broken legs and the other one killed himself," Sophie said sarcastically.

"That's what that cop wanted you to believe," Murphy said. "But both died with crusty black scorch marks around their eyes."

"Just like Marty," Sophie breathed.

"Your friend had been visited by the wolves," Murphy grunted.

"Impossible, I was with him just before he died," Sophie explained. "I would have remembered."

"You told me that you had fallen asleep and woken to find him staggering into the road," I reminded her. "He could have been visited by a wolf while you slept."

"But why burn out Marty's eyes and not mine?" she pondered. "It doesn't make sense."

"Does anything make sense anymore?" I said, glancing at Murphy in his carpet slippers.

"Perhaps they wanted your friend Marty to tell them about the blood," Murphy said. "Tell them what he had discovered."

"I guess," Sophie said thoughtfully, but I could tell that she wasn't convinced. It was like something was troubling her – something she couldn't quite remember.

Then, from not too far away came the sound of howling, and we all turned to look at each other. At first I wondered if it was just the wind screaming up the hill. But as it got closer, I recognised the sound to be that of wolves.

18

Sophie

Something wasn't quite right and it wasn't just the sound of the wind howling around the tumbled down farmhouse. Potter and this police officer – if that's what he really was – seemed to be convinced that Marty had been killed by one of the Skin-walkers, staring into his eyes, hoping to find out what he had discovered while testing Kiera Hudson's blood.

But as they stood and tried to convince me, my flesh turned cold, breaking out in tiny goose bumps. Somewhere in the back of my mind I could hear the sound of someone chuckling. Then they spoke, as if whispering into my ear.

"Oh, Sophie," the voice said.

Then, like a broken reflection in a cracked mirror, I saw a long, pointed face looking back at me. His cheeks and eye sockets were sunk deep into his face, like caves. He wore a navy blue baseball cap on his head and a red bandanna was tied about his scrawny throat. But it was his eyes. They burnt in his face, like two seething suns.

Who are you? I whispered, inside my mind.

"It doesn't matter," he smiled back, his lips a twisted scar. "You won't remember me."

Then he was gone, snuffed out like a light bulb inside my head.

Murphy was shouting at Potter again.

"Help me wedge this against the door!" he roared, nudging a woodworm-infested cupboard across the room with his dodgy hip.

Potter lifted one end off the floor and pressed it against the door. Then, looking at the guy with the pipe hanging from his mouth like a child's soother, he said, "I don't want to piss all over another one of your plans, Sarge, but a few armchairs and cupboards aren't going to stop those wolves."

"Got a better plan?" Murphy shouted over the sound of the howling and the barking that was growing ever closer outside.

"Well anything's got to be better than this," Potter snapped back, pointing at the flimsy-looking cupboard they had pushed against the front door.

"What's wrong with my plans?" Murphy asked, yanking the pipe from the corner of his mouth and staring at Potter.

"Well, for starters, what about when you had us dress up in disguise at Hallowed Manor..." Potter started.

"That was a great plan," Murphy cut in. "It would have worked if it hadn't have been for you!"

"For me?" Potter said in disbelief.

"You wrapped bandages around your head for fuck's sake! That was never part of the plan!" Murphy roared, as the howling grew louder from outside. "Jesus, you were prancing about the place like the Invisible Man on crack!"

"I've never done any crack," Potter shot back.

"Yeah?" Murphy said. "You could've fooled me."

With the sounds of snarling and howling just outside the door, I stared in disbelief at Potter and his friend and said, "Are you two going to stand there bitching at each other all night long or -" but before I'd the chance to finish, one of the chairs that Murphy had placed in front of the window flew across the room in a shower of glass.

Unable to stop myself, I let out an ear-piercing scream as a giant black snout poked its way through the window and sniffed at the air in the room.

As if I hadn't made a sound, Potter pointed at the splintered armchair, and looking at Murphy, he said, "See, I told you it wouldn't work."

The wolf forced its colossal skull through the window, tearing out the frame in a shower of brick and dust. Thick lengths of foamy, white drool swung from its jaws as it howled in fury. Working its claws through the hole it had created, the wolf tried to scramble into the farmhouse. Moving so quickly that he seemed like a blur, Potter shot from where he had been arguing with Murphy and was now attacking the giant wolf.

Potter's claws were like a set of knives as he slashed and ripped at the wolf. The creature howled in agony, and its breath was so strong that my hair blew back off my shoulders. From the foot of the stairs, I watched as Potter wrestled with the beast as it fought its way into the room. I glanced at Murphy as the front door began to shake in its frame. The sound of crashing was deafening as the wolves outside threw themselves against the door, desperate to get at us. Murphy stood before the door, and I watched with my mouth open wide as he slowly unbuttoned his police shirt, and placed it neatly to one side. I had called him a granddad, but in fact, with his shirt off, he looked anything but. His body was pale and slender, and what meat he did have on him was toned with muscle. He had the body that any twenty-year-old guy could only dream of having.

I glanced back at Potter, who was now on his back, kicking upwards at the gnashing jaws of the wolf. "Any time you feel like joining in will be fine with me," Potter yelled at his friend.

"Aren't you going to help him?" I shouted, unable to believe that Murphy seemed more interested in folding his shirt.

"Just got to kick off the old slippers," Murphy said, sucking on his pipe.

The front door was now hanging from its rusty hinges, and the sounds of the wolves' claws scratching against wood panels filled me with fear. I glanced at Potter; the wolf had managed to work one of its boulder-sized shoulders through the window and it was now swiping at Potter, who still lay on his back, driving the heel of his boot upwards into the jaws of the beast.

If Murphy seemed to be taking his time in helping Potter, I knew that I just couldn't stand by and watch him fight for his life. Spinning around, I looked for anything that I could use as a weapon. I spied the broken armchair and raced across the room, and gritting my teeth together I wrenched free one of its legs. It came away in my hand, jagged and sharp, looking like a giant stake.

Now that the wolf had its head just inches from Potter, I got a true understanding of the size of it. Its head was as big as a bear, but it was sleeker looking and its eyes blazed yellow. Its ears pointed upwards and silver whiskers sprung from its dripping snout. Charging across the room, I brought the stake up above my head; then, with all my strength, I sliced it down through the air in a sweeping arc and buried the splintered point into the top of its skull. There was a crunching sound as the wolf's skull fractured. Gripping the stake with both hands, I forced the splintered chair leg deep into the wolf's head. Blood jetted from its nostrils in thick, ropey streams and splattered the floor. The wolf jerked its head left and right and made a howling noise deep in the back of its throat.

Seeing that the wolf was panicked and in pain, Potter leapt to his feet, burying his fangs into the wolf's throat. The wolf paddled its mighty claws in the air as it frantically tried to knock Potter away. But with every swipe, it began to lose strength until it finally fell still, hanging half in and half out of the window like a blood-stained rug.

Potter withdrew his fangs from the wolf's throat, and wiping away the blood and fur from his chin, he looked at me and said, "Thanks."

I pulled the stake from the beast's head, and as it came away, it made a sickening squelching sound that made me want to puke. Standing by the window with blood dripping from the jagged tip of the chair leg, I watched the wolf shrink in shape and lose its fur as it returned back to its human form. The body that now lay bleeding on the floor was that of a young female. It was difficult to tell exactly how old she had been, as by removing the stake from her head, a loose piece of scalp had fallen across her face. Her naked skin was smooth and creamy white and I guessed she couldn't have been too much older than myself.

Before I'd had any chance to feel pity for the human woman that she had once been before being matched with the wolf, the front door exploded inwards in a shower of razor-sharp splinters. I spun around to see Murphy fly backwards into the stairs, the banisters snapping like matchsticks. Before

Murphy had even hit the ground, a set of black leathery-looking wings sprung from his back. With a set of fangs and claws that a prehistoric monster would have been proud of, Murphy launched himself at the wolves that were now scrambling over one other, desperate to get inside the farmhouse.

Potter saw the wolf before I did, and with a sweep of his arm, he set me spinning backwards towards the fire. With the heat of the fire prickling at my skin, I watched the wolf clatter into the wall, where I'd been standing only moments before. Dragging myself to my feet, I watched as both Murphy and Potter set about the wolves as they charged through the door. They moved with such lightning speed, that it was almost impossible to see them. They became nothing but a series of shadows as they flitted about the room. Clumps of wolf fur and flesh sprayed up into the air and stuck to the wall like jelly. With my stomach lurching, I watched the lumps of meat slowly slide down the damp-ridden farmhouse walls and splat onto the floor in raw-looking piles. The howling, barking, and snarling filled the room, and it was so loud it was like someone had cranked up the bass. Their growls vibrated off the walls and made me tremble.

Through the haze of blood and shadows, I caught fleeting glances of Potter and Murphy as they hacked, sliced, and bit their way through the wolves. Despite their constant bickering they now worked as a team – a team that had trained hard together over many years. It was almost like each would anticipate the move of the next. Potter would lunge one way, as Murphy kicked and ripped in the other. For the first time that night, Murphy didn't look or act like some old grandfather with his pipe and comfy slippers. As I watched him fight, I realised that Murphy was a sleek predator, designed to kill, as was Potter.

As the butchery continued all around me, a wolf broke free of the fight. It rolled onto the floor before the fire, and I couldn't tell which burnt more fiercely, the hissing knots of wood, or the wolf's eyes. Spotting me, the wolf rolled its foaming pink tongue around its snout and came towards me. With his ears pinned backwards, he snarled and leapt into the air. I raised the stake before me, but I was too slow, and the wolf pawed it from me. With the window behind me as my only means of escape, I gripped the arms of the girl hanging half in and out of the window and pulled. There was a tearing sound, as her stomach snagged on a shard of glass that stuck from the window frame like a broken tooth. With the wolf snarling at my heels, I hoisted the dead female from the window, where she rolled across the floor to the wolf. Smelling the fresh blood, the wolf paused and dragged its fleshy pink tongue across the loose flap of scalp that still covered her face. Throwing my hands to my face, I watched as the wolf buried its snout into the opening of her skull and began to lap up her brains.

Unable to watch, I knew that while the wolf paused to feed, I had a few precious moments in which to make my escape, so I scrambled out of the window. The cold night air hit me like a slap in the face and within moments, my nose had started to turn numb. From inside the farmhouse, I could hear the continued roars and snarls as Potter and Murphy continued to fight the wolves. Now that I was free of the farmhouse, I looked around for somewhere to hide. The moon was high in the sky and made the long grass shine as if it had been sprayed with silver. On the other side of the farmhouse I could see the silhouette of the burnt-out barn. Then, there was a scratching sound coming from behind me. I glanced back to see the wolf who I'd escaped from leaning out of the window. Its snout glistened in the moonlight, smeared with the brains of the dead Skin-walker. It sniffed the air; then, as if finding my scent on the wind, it turned and looked at me with its seething eyes. Howling, it bounded from the window and raced towards me.

Blind with panic, I screamed Potter's name as I raced away from the farmhouse and back along the coastal path that weaved its way down Black Hill. My heart felt as if it were going to explode in my chest as the long, brown coat and tree-hugger dress flew out behind me and I raced along the path. The sound of the wolf's breathing thundered behind me, and I started to cry with fear. With my arms working like pistons, I raced forward, drawing in lungfuls of icy cold air. I wanted to scream for Potter again, but I just couldn't draw enough breath into my lungs.

The wolf was so close now that I felt its teeth snag at my dress, and I stumbled forward. That was all that the wolf needed, and I felt the weight of its paws on my shoulders as it dragged me to the ground. I lay there waiting for its ferocious jaws to sink into me, when suddenly it felt as if it had disappeared. I rolled over in the grass to see the wolf soaring away from me and up into the sky. Screwing up my eyes, I just caught sight of Potter and his pointed wings as he dragged the wolf upwards and away from me.

"Run Sophie, run!" Potter roared.

I staggered to my feet and not knowing in which direction I was heading, I just ran. With the sound of the wolf howling high above me, I raced across an open field. The ground was uneven, and I stumbled and fell as I made my way across it. In the distance I could see a slate stone wall. Believing that it would offer me a place to hide, I headed towards it, all the while the wolf barking and woofing overhead as Potter fought with it.

I reached the wall, and hitching up my dress, I scrambled over it. I found myself standing on a hard surface, completely different to that of the field that I had just raced across. I looked right and could see that I was standing in the middle of a narrow country road. I glanced left, and that's when I saw the car bearing down on me. It was swerving left and right, but before I'd had a chance to dart out of its way, it hit me and I was spinning through the air. Then everything went black.

19

Potter

The wolf's blood sprayed into my mouth and it was hot and sticky. It dribbled off my chin and splashed onto my chest. It made one last swipe at me with its claw, which swished over my head. Thrusting my claw into his chest, I gripped its beating heart and popped it. With it twitching in my arms, I ripped out its heart and watched as it spiralled away from me back towards the ground, its tail jerking from side to side. Throwing its heart over my shoulder, I looked into the distance to see Sophie racing away into the dark, and I went after her.

With my wings folding backwards, I lost altitude and skimmed just inches above the field towards her. The wind snagged at my hair, and as I sped towards her, I saw Sophie scramble over a wall that lined the edge of the field. Glancing to my left, I saw two cones of bright light racing through the dark and the sound of a car engine revving at speed. I looked back at Sophie and saw the danger she was in. I opened my mouth to call her, but before the words had even worked their way up my throat, the car struck her. As if in slow motion, I watched Sophie cartwheel over the bonnet of the car and land on the road with a sickening thud.

"*No!*" I roared, bracing my wings, and landing in the field on the opposite side of the wall from where Sophie now lay motionless in the road. The car screeched to a halt, and I started over the wall. Then, I was grabbed from behind and thrown into the ditch.

"No, Potter," Murphy growled in my ear. "You'll be seen."

"I have to help her," I hissed, pushing him away from me.

"Look!" Murphy snapped, pointing over the wall as he crouched behind it.

On my knees, I peered through the brambles and nettles that lined the wall. A man climbed from the vehicle and walked back up the road towards Sophie's body. He lent over the body, as if examining her. Then, the passenger door flew open and a teenage girl staggered onto the road. She fell to her knees, and then losing a shoe, she stood and weaved her way up the road towards the man and Sophie. I could see that the young girl was pissed.

"They'll help her," Murphy whispered. "Now let's go."

"I can't just leave her," I said.

"Potter, we can't risk being seen," he snapped at me.

"I can hide my wings and claws. I could look like one of them."

"We can't risk being seen with or without wings. It won't be long before more Skin-walkers come and find the bloodbath that we've left up at that farm," Murphy insisted. "If these people see us, then they might..."

"I've got to help her," I told him, looking into his bright blue eyes.

"Find a way of *pushing* the world back," Murphy said, "and you will help her. None of this would ever have happened, and Sophie will go back to being that young woman who was studying music, the woman who ignored your letters..."

"But can we *push* it back?" I asked him, desperate to know the answer.

"I don't know," Murphy stared back at me. "But we've got to try. Not just for Sophie's sake, for all of our sakes."

"What do you mean?" I asked, as the man on the other side of the wall started to shout at the drunken girl.

"Let me show you," Murphy whispered, as he started to crawl away from the wall and back towards the farmhouse.

"But Sophie..."

"If you want to help her, we need to *push* back," Murphy said over his shoulder.

I glanced one last time over the wall, but Sophie's lifeless body was hidden from me by the man and the drunken girl who stood over her. There was a part of me that was glad I could no longer see her. I didn't want to remember her lying face-up in the road, her arms and legs splayed at unnatural angles from where the car had crushed her body. Turning away, and hoping Murphy was right about being able to help Sophie by pushing the world back, I followed him up the hill.

Careful not to step in the fur-covered remains of the wolves that Murphy and I had slain, I made my way across the living room. I snatched up the rucksack that I had taken from Kiera's flat. In it, I found one of Sophie's dresses, her iPod, and the letters that had somehow seeped through into this world. Holding them in my hands, I looked at Murphy and said, "I sent these to Sophie before I died and came back."

"I know you did," he said. "I found them while you were in her room and read them. I know all about you and Sophie."

"You read them?" I glared.

"Yeah," Murphy shrugged and carried on buttoning up his shirt. "I think parts of this world are overlapping – *merging* – with the world we once knew."

"What do you mean?" I asked him.

"Those letters shouldn't be here," he said, sliding his feet back into his slippers. "Imagine laying a piece of tracing paper over a map of the world. You make an exact copy, but then you move that piece of tracing paper to the right – just a fraction. It still looks like the world, but you can still see the one underneath; however faint, it's still there. Well, that's what I think has happened. Someone has moved the tracing paper but didn't expect the world underneath to start shining through. Get it?"

"I think so," I said, looking down at the envelopes with the smudged ink on them. It did look as if my handwriting was hidden beneath a piece of tracing paper.

"Those letters slowly made Sophie remember you," Murphy said. "Then when you showed up, she remembered completely. It was as if her two worlds had been merged, laid on top of one another."

I looked up from the letters and stared at Murphy.

"Get your stuff together," he said. "I want to show you something."

"What?"

"Just get your stuff," he ordered, and left the farmhouse.

I placed the picture of Kiera and her father in the bottom of the rucksack along with her police badge and the roll of money I had taken from the cookie jar. Over these, I placed the small amount of clothes I'd managed to swipe before the Skin-walkers had shown up at her flat. I took Sophie's iPod and earphones and placed them in my jeans pocket. Then, I picked up her dress, rolled the letters up inside it and tossed them into the fire. I stood for a moment and watched it start to burn. Like Murphy had said, those letters had no business being in this world. They were written in another *where* – in another *when*.

I put on the scarecrow's coat, turned my back on the fire, and left the farmhouse.

20

Potter

We raced through the night sky and it felt great to be flying alongside Murphy again. I'd missed his friendship, even if he could be an annoying old fart at times. I couldn't wait to take him back to the manor; Kiera and the others wouldn't believe who I had found again – although I got the feeling *he* had found *me*. The thought of having the old team back together again made me feel, for the first time, that coming back from the dead hadn't been so bad after all. But the old team, the one we had before wouldn't be the same, as there was someone missing.

Murphy dropped through the night and I followed. The very first rays of the morning sun lit the underbellies of the rain clouds that were starting to form around us. I raced alongside Murphy and could see the spire of a church some way off in the distance and we headed towards it. I glanced sideways at Murphy, and his face looked grim, as if there was something troubling him, and I knew there was stuff about this world that he had yet to tell me.

With our wings arching behind us like giant black sails, we dropped out of the sky and landed in the grounds of the church with the spire, which shone like a giant needle in the dawn light. Dead leaves rustled amongst the gravestones that lay before us in neat rows. Some of the headstones looked ancient and tilted to the right, more green than grey now where moss had spread over them. The early morning was quiet, and only the sound of the wind could be heard as Murphy led me to a small plot of land at the back of the graveyard. There was a tree with twisted black branches and roots that poked up through the ground like snakes.

"Where are we going?" I whispered, the rucksack swinging from my fist.

"Shhh!" he said. "Show some respect, we're amongst the dead here."

"We are dead, remember?"

Ignoring me, Murphy weaved his way amongst the headstones, his wings brushing against the fallen leaves. Beneath the tree, he came to a sudden stop between two small headstones. Unlike most of the others that we had passed, these were newer-looking and didn't have the moss and ivy covering them. Murphy remained silent as I read the names that had been chiselled into the headstone.

The first read *Kayla Hunt* and the second *Isidor Hunt*.

Feeling as if I'd been punched in the stomach, I looked at Murphy and said, "I thought Isidor's surname was *Smith*."

"He was raised with his sister here," Murphy said, his head bowed, as if in respect.

"What happened to them?" I asked, and although I knew both Kayla and Isidor were both safe and well back at Hallowed Manor, I couldn't help but feel a massive sense of loss – it was like I was grieving for them all over again, just like I had in The Hollows.

"They were both murdered," Murphy said, his cold, blue eyes fixed on their graves.

"I know that, I was there," I told him. "Luke murdered them."

"Elias Munn," he said bitterly.

"Yes," I said. "He fooled all of us. Luke..."

"I don't want to speak of him," Murphy barked. "He sold us all out, and was the person behind the deaths of my daughters."

"And your death," I reminded him.

Then turning to face me, he said, "You were right about Jack Seth. I should have listened to you."

To hear Murphy say that – to give me credit at long last – made me feel that I had finally achieved something, and that I was not a no-hoper after all. I couldn't tell him how those few words of his made me feel, but I would never forget them. "Thanks," I said to him.

"For what?" he asked, cocking one of his silver eyebrows.

"It doesn't matter," I said, then added, "So what happened to them here?"

"They weren't murdered by Elias Munn here," Murphy said. "They were murdered by their father, Lord Hunt."

"Get the fuck out of here!" I gasped.

"Shut your filthy mouth! You're in a graveyard, for fuck's sake!" Murphy shot back at me.

"But you just said the 'F' word too, didn't you?"

"Look, Potter, I'm in no mood for trick questions," Murphy snapped at me. "Do you want to know what happened to our friends here or not?"

"Of course I do," I told him.

Taking his pipe, and knocking out the old ash against Isidor's headstone, Murphy started to explain what had happened to our friends. "Lord Hunt was a scientist, just like we knew him to be. But most people thought him to be just some crazy old man. He believed that winged demons lived beneath the earth."

"Not so crazy," I said, watching Murphy push a lump of tobacco into his pipe and light it.

"Not to us perhaps," he said, "but to the people in this world, his theories were just insane ramblings. His wife wasn't as crazy, but over time he got her to come around to his way of thinking. Lord Hunt believed that these winged demons were building an army, which would rise up out of the ground and attack the humans. He thought they would join forces with the wolves and destroy the human race – if they didn't turn them all into vampires first by feeding off them. So convinced was he by his theory, that he spent his life's work designing a synthetic blood, which by chance – or not – he called Lot 13."

"So that's why there are bottles and bottles of the stuff left at the manor," I said. "So where are Lord and Lady Hunt now?"

"I'm coming to that, be patient, Potter," he mumbled as he sucked on his pipe. "Lord and Lady Hunt had two children, Kayla and Isidor. As they grew up, Hunt, in his paranoid state, began to suspect that his children were, in fact, winged demons sent from beneath ground to start the infiltration of the human race. When his wife refused to follow him down this path, he became suspicious of her, suspecting that she had been impregnated by one of these winged demons, who he believed lived below ground.

"Of course, no one believed in his insane ramblings, and he spent some time incarcerated in mental institutions. While Hunt was locked away, his children flourished and lived semi-normal lives, both attending boarding schools, as their mother often struggled to cope on her own. Just a few weeks before their deaths, Lord Hunt was released and considered fit and well to return home, his delusional state now under control with the aid of medication. But he had only been home a few weeks when the paranoia returned. He started to argue with his wife, accusing her again of falling pregnant to one of these winged demons. Then, one night, as Lady Hunt slept restlessly in her bed, Lord Hunt crept into her room and slit her throat. Knowing that he would suffer the death penalty unless he proved to the world his wife's adultery and the existence of the winged demons, he took his two children up into the mountains.

"Telling Isidor and Kayla that their mother was in bed with a fever and needed to rest, he invited them to join him on a short camping trip up into the Cambrian Mountains. Believing that their father had been cured, and both desperate to spend time with him, they went willingly with him up into the mountains. After setting up camp for the night, they ate their supper by the fire. But unbeknown to both Isidor and Kayla, Lord Hunt had laced their food with a strong tranquiliser. It wasn't long before both had fallen into a deep sleep by the fire.

"Desperate to prove to the world that he wasn't mad, and that both of his children were, in fact, demons from the underworld, he took the surgical knives that he had hidden in his sleeping bag and murdered both Kayla and Isidor. He worked on Isidor first, slicing open his back and removing his spine in search of the wings that he believed were hidden inside his son. When he failed to find any, he turned to his daughter. The attack on her was brutal – savage. He opened up her back, looking for clawed wings that he was sure were hidden inside of her. When he failed to find them, he cut off her ears, believing that he would find pointed ones underneath. But there were none. He then removed her teeth, desperately in search of fangs. He pulled out her fingernails with a pair of pliers, looking for her claws.

"With Kayla's body scattered about him, he sunk into a total fit of madness. Panicking, he wrapped Kayla's remains in her sleeping bag and dragged her up the mountainside, believing that he might be able to hide the bodies. But even in his deluded state, he must have known that his efforts were pointless. His wife lay dead back at the manor, her throat slit open, and his two children lay hacked to pieces and scattered over the mountain.

"Lady Hunt was eventually found a week later by a friend of the family. There had been a heavy snow during that time and Kayla's remains were eventually discovered a week later, then her brother's almost two weeks after that. Eventually Lord Hunt was found frozen to death, ten miles from where he had left Kayla's body. It's believed that he walked aimlessly into the blizzard and died of hypothermia," Murphy said.   "So, in the same way they were murdered in The Hollows, they were murdered here, too," I said, looking down at their graves. "But while they were both murdered *there* by Luke, *here* they were murdered by their father."

"Just like I said," Murphy grunted. "Almost the same, but different – *pushed* somehow. But Kayla and Isidor must never find out what happened to them here – they shouldn't even be *here!*"

"So why have you shown me this?" I asked him, frowning.

"This isn't the sole reason I brought you here," Murphy said, "there is something else."

Without saying another word and keeping close to the trees, Murphy led me around the edge of the graveyard. We hadn't gone very far when he flapped his hand at me, signalling me to get down. I crouched behind a gravestone that tilted slightly to the right and peered over the top.

"What am I meant to be looking at?" I whispered to Murphy, who was hiding behind a gravestone to my left.

With the pipe hanging from the corner of his mouth, Murphy pointed into the distance. From my hiding place, I looked in the direction he was pointing and saw a man standing alone in the middle of the graveyard. He was staring down at one of the headstones. He was tall, with black hair that was swept back from his brow. It was as I looked at his drawn and ashen face that I recognised him, and my stomach knotted. The man I was spying on was Kiera's father. Hadn't he died of cancer a few years back? I wondered.

I shot a look at Murphy and as if reading my thoughts, he whispered. "He is still very much alive here."

Turning my head, I peered over the top of the grave again and watched as he gently rested a tiny bunch of flowers on top of the headstone; he then lent forward and kissed it. With his head cast down, he turned and walked slowly back across the graveyard. When he had gone, Murphy stood up and rubbed the small of his back with his hands.

"C'mon," he said.

As I set off after him, I started to fear what it was that he wanted to show me.

Murphy stood before the headstone, and not wanting to look at the name carved into the face of it, I stared at the flowers that Kiera's father had left behind. Some of the petals broke loose in the wind and scattered over the grave like confetti.

"Look at the grave," Murphy whispered.

"I am," I said.

"Look at the name."

"I can't."

"You have to."

Lowering my eyes, I looked down at the headstone, and read the name written across it: *Kiera Hudson.* It made me feel sad to look at her name, and although I knew Kiera was dead – she wasn't to me; she was still very much alive.

"How did she die?" I whispered, now unable to tear my eyes from her grave. The smell of his tobacco smoke made me half-crazy for a cigarette, but I couldn't, not here.

"In this world, Kiera was similar to the Kiera we know and love. She was a twenty-year-old rookie cop. She lived just around the corner from the flat where she once lived, but you know that already."

"So apart from her father still being alive, what else is different?"

"Kiera was shot in the line of duty while attending a robbery," Murphy explained. "It was no big deal in this world, as cops die all the time; it didn't even make the newspapers."

"But I thought her body was discovered on the side of a mountain, just like the others," I said, feeling confused.

"A completely different mountain," Murphy said. "Miles from where Kayla and Isidor were discovered. Her death was never connected to theirs. Besides, apart from your friend Sophie, no one knew the name of the body that was brought down from the side of that mountain. As far as this world is concerned – Kiera Hudson, the young rookie cop, was shot in the line of duty. No one really cared, the robber was human, so no Treaty conflicts there, and every morning before setting off to work, her broken-hearted father comes and lays flowers on her grave."

"What about her mother?" I asked him.

"She died giving birth to Kiera," Murphy told me. "Her father raised his daughter on his own. She meant everything to him."

"But Kiera will want to see her father – she loves him – she made him a promise..." I started.

"No!" Murphy snapped. "She must never find out that her father is still alive here."

"So why have you brought me here?"

"You must make sure that she never finds out, Potter," he said. "If Kiera finds out that her father is still alive, then like you say, she will want to see him, speak with him, it would only be natural. But she can't. Our Kiera is not *his* Kiera."

"They come from two different *whens*," I said, trying to make sense of everything.

"Exactly," Murphy grunted. "And what if Kiera were to meet her father? Would she then want to push the world back and lose him all over again?"

"But I can't keep a secret like that from her," I told him. "She has a right to know that her father is still alive."

"She has no rights!" Murphy glared. "She doesn't have the right to be here – none of us do."

"So why are we here?" I snapped back at him.

"Beats the shit out of me," Murphy said. "But until we figure out why we are here, none of us must get involved with our past lives.

"Like me and Sophie?"

"Yeah, just like you and Sophie," he said. "Look what happened. She remembered you. All those feelings she had for you weren't really her feelings. They were the feelings of the Sophie from the world trying to shine through the tracing paper. Those feelings that she suddenly had, broken memories and half dreams, would have driven her mad in the end. This world is all that these people know and care about. Kiera's father believes his daughter is dead, and she is, as far as this world is concerned. What would happen if he knew that she was living again on the other side of the country? It's not her – it's not the Kiera that you are in love with; it's the Kiera who was brought up in a world where wolves live amongst humans. It's a world where she is dead."

"I don't know if I can keep something like this from her," I said.

"You must keep her away from her old life, Potter," he warned. "If her father should see her, then perhaps the world will merge just a little bit more, then a little bit more, and I fear that could be catastrophic for all of us."

"How come?"

"I think Lord Hunt went mad because some part of him remembered the Vampyrus. Perhaps on a subconscious level, he knew that he had been a Vampyrus. Remember, he couldn't be taken back into The Hollows because he died above ground.

Maybe this world and the other one started to merge and it sent him mad. We know what he was babbling on about is true. There was a race of winged demons living below ground – us, Potter. What if enough people start to remember their other existence? What if the Vampyrus were to come back into this world? What would the world be like then? We've got to find a way of pushing that sheet of tracing paper back into place – get things back to how they were. So you can't risk Kiera, Kayla, or Isidor finding out what happened to them here."

"But I don't want to keep secrets from my friends, especially not from Kiera," I told him. "She would hate me if she found out that her father was still alive and I hadn't told her."

"Then you better make sure that she never finds out," Murphy said with a grim look on his face. "If Kiera even suspected that her dad was still alive, the need to see him would be unbearable, I should know."

"What do you mean?" I quizzed.

"My wife and daughters are still alive here," he said, and looked away into the distance. "I'm not, I'm dead. But they are alive, not very far from here."

"How do you know?" I breathed.

"Just like Kiera wouldn't be able to resist, I had to go and see them for myself. It's okay, they didn't see me. But to watch Chloe, Meren, and Nessa, broke my fucking heart. Knowing that they were alive, but unable to go to them was enough to drive me insane. I'm Chloe's husband and Meren's and Nessa's dad. But not here. I might look like him in every way, but I'm not him and they're not mine. If I were to have contact with them, they might start to remember how they truly died, in that hospital, hidden in the attic at Hallowed Manor. Would their dreams become haunted with images of them as half-breeds? And what of Chloe, she had died – would she die here, too?"

"But if we push the world back, then won't your daughters go back to being half-breeds – aren't they dead in our world? Aren't we all dead?"

"This world wasn't meant to be, Potter, that's why I believe the other is trying to seep through," Murphy said, pumping grey clouds of smoke from his pipe. "It's like it's trying to right itself in some way – but with disastrous consequences."

"So why did the Elders do this?" I asked.

"I don't know," he said, shaking his head. "Was this their plan? Did they intend for this to happen? Or was it a mistake?"

"What did they say when they brought you back?"

"Basically they said I was a prick for trusting Jack Seth, and an even bigger prick for releasing him from prison," he moaned. "And I guess they were right – just like you had been."

"So they are punishing you for that?"

"So it would seem," he said thoughtfully. "But maybe none of this is a punishment; maybe it's a test, or perhaps even another chance."

"Another chance at what?"

"At not screwing up again," he half-smiled at me.

I looked down at Kiera's grave again, then staring back at Murphy, I said, "I don't like this – I'm not happy about keeping secrets from Kiera."

Then, staring hard back at me, Murphy said, "So you're gonna be telling Kiera how you met up with Sophie again?"

"That's not fair!" I snapped.

"I guess that's exactly what Kiera would say if she ever found out," he said back, and then added, "Sometimes it's best to keep a secret. Not because we want to deceive those we love, but because we just want to protect them."

Tipping out the ash from his pipe, Murphy turned and headed away. I glanced one last time at Kiera's grave and went after him. Beneath the tree with the black knotted roots, I looked at my friend and said, "Although I feel as if you've just shit on me from a great height, I'm glad that you're back. I know the others will be knocked out to see you again."

"I'm not coming back to the manor with you," he said. "You can't tell them about me."

"Why aren't you coming back?" I frowned.

"I've got work to do," he said. "I've wormed my way back into the police, into a position where I can perhaps figure out a way of sorting this mess out."

"Why can't I tell the others that you're back?"

"Because it could blow my cover. The fewer people that know my true identity, the better," he said.

"But they wouldn't tell anyone about you if you asked them not to," I tried to convince him.

"Not willingly, perhaps," Murphy said, "but it would only take one of those Skin-walkers to do that thing with their eyes, and Kiera and the others wouldn't have to say anything."

"So why show yourself to me?"

"I hadn't planned to, but when the girl Sophie told me that she had seen a girl with flaming red hair and a guy with a crossbow, I knew who she was talking about. And if Kayla and Isidor were back, then I knew you would be somewhere close by."

"So?" I said. "That still doesn't explain why you came after me. You haven't gone after Kayla, Isidor, or Kiera."

"Like I tried to explain earlier, just like Kiera wouldn't be able to resist searching for her father if she knew he was alive..." then, looking as if he wanted to continue but couldn't, he looked at me and said, "I'll be in touch."

Murphy opened his wings, looked at me one last time, then shot into the sky. Within seconds, I heard a rumble of thunder, and I couldn't be sure if it had been caused by Murphy speeding away or by an oncoming storm.

21

Potter

I flew away in the opposite direction to Murphy and headed back towards Hallowed Manor. When I was a few miles away, the menacing clouds, which swirled around me, started to shed their rain. I rolled over, flying on my back, enjoying the feel of it against my face. I clutched the rucksack in one hand and it buffeted from side to side in the wind. Once I could see the manor on the horizon, I dropped through the sky, soared low over the moat, and landed in the wooded area not too far from the summerhouse. I ditched the scarecrow's coat and let the rain wash the Skin-walker's blood from my chest, arms, and hands.

Taking shelter beneath the willow trees, I propped myself against a trunk and lit a cigarette. I breathed in deeply and then blew out the smoke which lingered beneath the overhanging branches of the tree. I opened up the rucksack and removed the picture of Kiera and her father. They looked so happy together in it. As usual, Kiera's beautiful hazel eyes stared out of the photograph, and although I thought I was looking at Kiera, I knew I wasn't really. I had never met this Kiera and even if I did, she wouldn't know me? That felt weird. Was there another Potter out there somewhere? I hoped not, but chances were that there was. Did I want to find him? No. *One Potter was enough for anyone*, I smiled to myself and smoked my cigarette.

I felt bad that I knew Kiera's father was alive, and although I had kind of got my head around the reason why I couldn't tell her, it didn't make it easier. I placed the picture back in the rucksack and closed it. Then, I remembered I had Sophie's iPod in my pocket. I pulled it out and switched it on. With the earphones dangling from my ears, I scrolled through the music tracks. I found the song *Fix You* by Coldplay and hit the play button with my thumb.

Leaning against the tree, I sat for a while, smoked, and listened to the song. As I sat there, I spied Kiera pass by on the other side of the overhanging branches. With the music still playing in my ears, I followed her. She made her way through the trees, unaware that I was there. I had been right when I'd told Sophie how beautiful Kiera was. She was more than beautiful, and for someone like me, it's so hard to explain how I feel about her. But one thing I did know – one thing that I could put down in words – I knew I never wanted to be without her.

Kiera stopped by the summerhouse and headed towards the statue which had appeared on the grass there. Did Murphy know about the statue? I knew that as always, there was going to be tough times ahead for me and my friends, and Kiera would be a big part of that. But whatever lay ahead, I would be at her side, shoulder to shoulder.

The music stopped. Thumbing through to the *settings* function, I wiped the iPod's memory, and with it, Sophie from my life once and for all. Placing the iPod back into my trouser pocket, I thought of Kayla and decided that I would give it to her as a present.

I threw the bag over my shoulder, stepped out into the rain and headed towards Kiera, who stood examining the statue in front of the summerhouse.

22

Sophie

I woke with a gasp. Where was I? It was warm and I could feel the sun on my face. There was a buzzing sound. I looked to my right and could see a wasp hovering beside me. I swished it away with the back of my hand. I pulled myself up, only to find that I had been lying in a ditch. There was a wide open field on one side of me and a wall made of slate on the other. I could smell the scent of freshly cut hay and it was wonderful. I pulled myself to my feet, and brushing mud from my dress, I looked over the wall. There was a road and it was then I remembered being hit by a car. How had I ended up in the ditch, I wondered, and where was Potter and that other guy? What had been his name? Murphy?

Wondering if they had gone back to the farmhouse, I made my way back across the field. Butterflies flittered back and forth. The last I could remember was that it had been cold, it had been winter. But now it was summer, how had the seasons changed so quickly?

As I made my way back up the hill, I soon realised the weather wasn't the only thing that had changed since being hit by that car. The disused barn that had once been burnt down now looked as if it was under construction. On the naked beams of the roof, I could see a well-built man in a checked shirt hammering corrugated sheets of metal into place. Keeping low so that he couldn't see me, I headed along the wall on the other side of the barn. I peered into the field and could see several tents and small caravans. It looked like the field had been turned into a small campsite. Still in search of Potter and his friend, Murphy, I continued upwards towards the farm. Just like before, the farmhouse was hidden from view by a small crop of trees. I took shelter from the sun in the shade and looked at the farmhouse. I was amazed to see that, although it still looked run down, it wasn't the derelict building that I could remember.

How had everything changed so much, I wondered, feeling confused and lost. Then, as I watched the farmhouse from beneath the trees, I saw a young girl appear from behind the front door. She strolled outside, wearing a yellow T-shirt and a short blue denim skirt. She couldn't have been any older than seventeen, and she was already very beautiful. I watched her flounce away down the path that led to the cliff edge. No sooner had I lost sight of her, when a boy with a baseball cap wedged on his head snuck from behind the front door and followed the girl down the path at a discreet distance.

It was then that I recognised the boy and the girl. I had seen them before on my walks up to the farm. I had often seen them sitting by the cliffs, staring into each other's eyes. And the girl and the big guy, the one building the barn, hadn't they been the people in the photograph I'd found in the bedroom? But what were they doing here now? Where had they come from and where was I?

Then, as if Potter was whispering in my ear, I heard him say, "I think it's more of a case of *when* you are, than *where* you are."

Stepping out from beneath the shade of the trees, I set off after the boy at a safe distance. But what if he saw me? What if that boy asked me who I was? I didn't know if the wolves were still looking for me. I had to be careful. Then feeling that plastic piece of I.D. in my pocket, I decided that until I figured out *when* I was, I would simply call myself Caroline Hughes.

'Dead Angels'

(Kiera Hudson Series Two)

Book 2
Now Available

More books by Tim O'Rourke

Vampire Shift (Kiera Hudson Series 1) Book 1
Vampire Wake (Kiera Hudson Series 1) Book 2
Vampire Hunt (Kiera Hudson Series 1) Book 3
Vampire Breed (Kiera Hudson Series 1) Book 4
Wolf House (Kiera Hudson Series 1) Book 4.5
Vampire Hollows (Kiera Hudson Series 1) Book 5
Dead Flesh (Kiera Hudson Series 2) Book 1
Dead Night (Kiera Hudson Series 2) Book 1.5
Dead Angels (Kiera Hudson Series 2) Book 2
Dead Statues (Kiera Hudson Series 2) Book 3
Dead Seth (Kiera Hudson Series 2) Book 4
Dead Wolf (Kiera Hudson Series 2) Book 5
Dead Water (Kiera Hudson Series 2) Book 6
Witch (A Sydney Hart Novel)
Black Hill Farm (Book 1)
Black Hill Farm: Andy's Diary (Book 2)
Doorways (Doorways Trilogy Book 1)
The League of Doorways (Doorways Trilogy Book 2)
Moonlight (Moon Trilogy) Book 1
Moonbeam (Moon Trilogy) Book 2
Vampire Seeker (Samantha Carter Series) Book 1

20559799R00077

Printed in Great Britain
by Amazon